DISTURBING
BEHAVIOR

DISTURBING BEHAVIOR

A NOVELIZATION

BY JOHN WHITMAN

BASED ON THE SCREENPLAY

BY SCOTT ROSENBERG

BANTAM BOOKS

New York • Toronto • London • Sydney • Auckland

ISBN 0-553-57139-7

Published simultaneously in the United States and Canada.

Bantam Books are published by Bantam Books, a division of Bantam Doubleday Dell Publishing Group, Inc. Its trademark, consisting of the words "Bantam Books" and the portrayal of a rooster, is Registered in U.S. Patent and Trademark Office and in other countries. Marca Registrada. Bantam Books, 1540 Broadway, New York, New York 10036.

PRINTED IN THE UNITED STATES OF AMERICA
OPM   10 9 8 7 6 5 4 3 2

PART ONE

Meet the musical little creatures

that hide among the flowers. . . .

CHAPTER 1

Andy Effkin and Mary Jo Copeland could see the ferry chugging across the bay. Or at least, they could have seen it if Mary Jo hadn't had her mouth plastered to Andy's in a serious liplock.

Mary Jo had made out with boys before. She figured she knew what they liked, so she went at it like the league MVP of kissing—her hands running through Andy's hair, her body pressed up against him, the works. She did all the things that drove the guys crazy, because that was what Mary Jo Copeland liked to do.

Except it wasn't working.

Andy Effkin just sat there pressed against the driver's side door of his father's car. Mary Jo frowned.

"So why'm I doing all the work here?" she said, sitting back with a pout.

Andy just shrugged.

Mary Jo shook her head. When Andy Effkin had asked her out she'd played it cool, but her knees had turned to instant pudding. Effkin was a major player at Cradle Bay High School. All-League football, straight-A student. She heard he even had perfect attendance. And he certainly had his pick of girls. He ought to have some experience with them—which was a lot more than she could say for the usual Wrestlemania rejects that tried to take her to the mat in the backseats of their fathers' cars. Andy had taken her on a real date: dinner, then dessert at the Yogurt Shoppe, then a trip up to the Bluffs for what she figured would be some furious face-crushing. Except he was suddenly turning out to be a dud in the stud department.

She sighed. Good face, hot bod, but about as interesting as a number two pencil.

"What's your deal?" she asked.

Finally Andy looked at her. "Big game Friday. It's no good. I need my fluids."

"Your fluids!" Mary Jo repeated, pouting again. "Thanks for the clue."

She leaned back and put her feet up on the dashboard. The move made her pant legs ride up a little, revealing a tattoo on her ankle. It was a picture of the devil, his face contorted in a permanent sneer, with the initials *M.J.C.* scrawled underneath.

Andy blinked. "Why would you do that?"

"What, the tattoo?" Mary Jo said. She flashed more leg and grinned. "Why not?"

Andy blinked again, as if he was thinking and it hurt. "But it's self-mutilation, really—"

"Hey," she said. "Self-mutilate this, fluid boy."

She threw her leg across his lap and started kissing him on the neck.

About thirty yards away and a little higher up in the woods, two pairs of eyes were watching as the car started to rock. One pair of eyes belonged to a border collie named Hysteria, who couldn't have cared less about Mary Jo, Andy's fluids, or the big game. But the other pair belonged to Gavin Strick, a lean, handsome seventeen-year-old who made it a point never to pass up the chance to make fun of the in crowd, even if there was no one around to hear the joke.

Besides, he had just finished smoking a cigarette packed with truly excellent marijuana, and he was in a good mood. There were only two reasons for teenagers to head up to the Bluffs. One was to make out. The other was to light up a joint and make fun of the ones making out.

"Andy Effkin," Gavin announced in his best sportscaster's voice. "The Toast with the Most. Ya gotta like this kid Effkin, Bob: the star quarterback prospect out of Cradle Bay High. He can throw a pass without interception—and make one without rejection."

Gavin shook his scruffy brown hair back from his eyes and held a nonexistent microphone to his mouth. "But ya gotta admit, Bob, they make an odd couple. Mary Jo Copeland, the tattooed lovely with an affinity for pills and poetry—and Andy E., the nineties prototype jockstrap meathead."

Gavin crept a little closer, keeping quiet and out of sight. The last thing he needed was to get mislabeled as a Peeping Tom. He had no desire to see Andy Effkin put his moves on anyone. But he was curious about why a girl like Mary Jo— who could actually think for herself—would go out with a Ken doll like Effkin.

Gavin took another step forward. He could just see them through the fogged-up windows of the car.

Inside the car, Andy Effkin opened his eyes as Mary Jo bit his neck. It was a playful nip, and when she felt him jump a little, she laughed and did it again.

A reaction at last.

If Mary Jo had looked up, she would have seen that Andy wasn't having nearly as good a time as she was. She would have seen his face go stone cold. His eyes, which had blinked so often earlier, suddenly stopped blinking altogether. In that moment something gleamed in the corner of one eye: a small, wedge-shaped chip that suddenly flashed.

"Slut," Andy murmured.

"Hmmm?" Mary Jo purred. "What'd you say?"

"Slut!" Andy repeated more loudly. He grabbed a fistful of Mary Jo's hair, making her neck arch backward. With his other hand he grabbed her by the chin. Then he twisted.

Mary Jo Copeland's neck broke with a loud snap.

From his vantage point, Gavin continued his monologue. The joke was going stale, but he didn't have anything better to do until he hooked up later with his friend U.V. and the rest of the gang.

Gavin saw Andy grab Mary Jo's hair. "Ooh, the jock likes the rough stuff," he said sarcastically. "Now there's a surprise."

Then he shut his mouth tight and leaned back against a tree. The blue and red lights of a police cruiser stained the air. The cruiser's siren let out a single loud whoop as the patrol car came to a stop a few feet behind Andy's father's car.

"Oh, no," Gavin whispered to himself. "The quarterback is thrown for a loss!"

Gavin recognized the two cops who got out. Officers Cox and Kramer. Citations of honor, respected family men, pillars of the community, blah, blah, blah. As far as Gavin was concerned, they were just two more slices in the loaf of processed white bread known as Cradle Bay.

Officer Cox strolled up to the car and tapped on the window.

"Hey, Andy," he said. "You want to step out of the car for a minute, Andy?"

Andy Effkin stepped out of the car, his face still a blank slate. But Officer Cox was all smiles. "So, you like your chances against Knight's Ridge this Friday?"

Andy nodded and mumbled, "Yes, sir."

Officer Kramer switched his flashlight on and casually played the light across the inside of the car.

Officer Cox said to Andy, "You know, you really shouldn't be out after curfew."

"Sonuvabitch!" Officer Kramer yelled, stumbling backward in surprise as Mary Jo's dead eyes stared up at him. "There's a dead girl in here!"

Before Officer Cox could react, Andy reached down and ripped the gun from the policeman's holster, leveled it at Kramer, and pulled the trigger. The bullet punched a hole in the policeman's chest and sent him flying backward. Dead on impact.

"Jesus!" Gavin whispered from his hiding place.

Officer Cox held out his hands, fingers spread, and said calmly, "Easy, Eff. Easy, buddy. Just calm down."

Andy Effkin glared at Officer Cox for a moment, the gun smoking in his hand. Then his shoulders slumped and he sighed.

Gavin watched as Cox stepped forward and gently removed the gun from the young man's hand.

"Well," Gavin concluded, "I'd say old Andy is about to get pulled from the game . . . for about twenty-five to life."

Gavin thought Officer Cox would slap the cuffs on Andy. He was shocked when the policeman simply holstered his gun, looked from Andy to Mary Jo to the blood-spattered corpse of his partner, and then said, "Get out of here, Andy. *Now*."

Gavin's jaw nearly hit the ground. "You've gotta be kidding me."

But it was no joke. Officer Cox didn't move a muscle as Andy Effkin dragged Mary Jo's body out of his car, dumped it on the ground, and got in. The policeman just watched as Andy Effkin started up the car and calmly drove away.

"Something's seriously wigged out here,"

Gavin whispered to his dog. "And you know what? I'm not sticking around to find out what it is."

He took off running.

CHAPTER 2

THE TEN BEST TOWNS TO RAISE A FAMILY

. . . Number two on our list of the ten best towns in the United States is Cradle Bay. Nestled in a sunny cove on an island in the Northwest, surrounded by green forests and covered by blue skies, Cradle Bay is a slice of old-fashioned America. The island (also called Cradle Bay) is only four miles off the coast, but it's a world away from the blights of urban sprawl. The crime rate is low, the average income is high, and just about everyone who lives there is on the straight and narrow.

Best of all, parents will find the schools in Cradle Bay some of the best in the country. Three years ago, test scores were above the national average, and they've only gone up. Whatever they're doing at Cradle Bay, they're obviously doing it right. . . .

★ ★ ★

Cynthia Clark set the magazine down on the wooden bench of the ferry. "You know," she said, "the more I read about this town, the more I like it."

Her husband, Nathan, smiled and handed her a cup of steaming coffee from a cardboard carrying tray. He handed another cup to their thirteen-year-old daughter, Lindsay. "Here's your hot chocolate, honey."

"Thanks, Dad," Lindsay said.

"You know, they have an indoor pool at the rec center," Mrs. Clark added. "You can swim all year round."

"Sounds great," Lindsay said. "Does Steve know? He likes to swim."

Her dad handed her the last cup from the tray. "Why don't you go tell him?"

Lindsay took the cup and carefully stood. The ferry rocked and rolled as it churned across the bay toward the distant island. Lindsay made her way from the inside sitting area to the deck, passing benches filled with passengers who sat reading the papers or tapping the keyboards of laptop computers. Obviously they were commuters who had seen the view a thousand times.

But to the Clarks it was all new, and Lindsay smiled as the wind blew her dark hair around. The dark water slapped at the bow of the ferry, and on the horizon the green island grew larger by the second.

Her brother, Steve, stood at the railing. He was a handsome seventeen-year-old with dark brown hair and a square jaw. Instead of looking ahead toward the island, he stared back at the mainland, watching as it grew smaller behind them. Lindsay tapped him on the shoulder and handed him the hot chocolate.

"I can't wait," she said. "Can't, cannot, *c-a-n-n-o-t* wait!"

Steve managed a smile. "To do what?"

Lindsay laughed. "See my new room. My new school. My new everything!"

Steve sighed. "Yeah. New everything."

"Don't you think it's thrilling?" his little sister asked him. "It's going to be better. I know it. *We're* going to be better."

Steve shrugged. He didn't want to put a damper on his sister's excitement. Most kids had trouble adjusting to a new environment, but Lindsay was taking it better than he was. Still, he couldn't help saying, "I hope you're right, Linds, but Mom and Dad are always telling us we can't just run away from our problems. And I feel like that's what we're doing."

Lindsay poked him in the ribs and was about to argue about the value of bigger bedrooms and indoor swimming pools when the ferry

bumped up against the dock. They hurried inside to find their parents. Together they all piled
into their car and waited in line for their turn
to drive off the boat. When they reached the
ramp that led onto the dock, they were stopped
by the ferryman, who took their ticket. He
glanced at the car packed full of suitcases and
duffel bags.

"Looks like you're moving to Cradle Bay," he
observed.

"Sure are," Mr. Clark replied.

The ferryman nodded. "Well, I'm sure you're
going to like it here. Safe to say you'll never want
to leave. Have a nice one."

He patted the hood of the car and waved
them on.

The highway led from the ferry dock through a
small forest of tall pine and spruce trees. Here
and there shafts of sunlight poked through the
forest canopy to the ground, forming columns of
pure light swirling with dust. Lindsay called
them fairy towers. Steve just shrugged.

The forest gave way suddenly to the town—a
neat collection of storefronts and small restau-
rants. They passed a yogurt shop and a record
store advertising PIANO LESSONS—FIRST HOUR
FREE! and were already leaving the tiny down-
town section of Cradle Bay and entering the

residential district, which had wide sidewalks and neatly trimmed lawns.

"Jeez," Steve whispered under his breath. "It's like driving through an episode of *Leave It to Beaver.*"

But even Steve perked up when they reached their new house. It was a tall two-story Victorian with a big front porch. His parents had promised him the house was big, and they hadn't been lying. It was twice the size of their house back in Chicago.

The moving van was waiting out front, and the Clark family plunged into the work of settling into their new home. There were boxes to open, dishes to put away, and beds to make— not to mention Mrs. Clark's continual rearranging of the furniture long after the moving men had left. Steve and his father must have shifted the sofa and the armchairs back and forth a dozen times over.

By the time most of their boxes had been unpacked, it was evening. Lindsay and her mom sat at the dining room table playing a game of Alien Autopsy while Mrs. Clark thought about what to cook for dinner. Steve was in his bedroom, poking through piles of books, CDs and audiotapes, unsure how to organize it all.

His father appeared in the doorway. "Hey, pal. You all right?"

Steve stood. "Yeah, yeah. Just trying to figure out if I really need all this stuff." He picked up a tape and grimaced. "You think I'll ever listen to Milli Vanilli again?" He chucked the tape into the trash bin.

His father laughed, then asked, "So, are you nervous?"

"About what?"

"Your first day of school. What else?"

Steve turned his back to his father and picked up a pile of loose photographs. He thought he ought to say something, but there was nothing to say. Steve was positive his dad wanted him to say he was fine, and that they had all left their troubles behind them in Chicago—as if Cradle Bay had put an impenetrable barrier between their old life and their new one. But Steve couldn't say that. It wasn't true. Still, he ought to say something. . . .

"Dad . . ." He turned to face his father, but Nathan Clark had already left the room.

Steve looked at one of the photos in his hand. It was a picture of him a few years earlier, playing football with his older brother, Allen. They were covered with mud and sweat, and they were grinning. Steve could remember the day and the hour of that meaningless, hilarious football game back in the park in Chicago. He had just slipped his brother's tackle and scored the winning points.

He could almost smell the wet grass and hear his brother's laughter.

But the memories of that football game seemed far away from their new home. Steve dropped the stack of photos in a desk drawer and shoved it closed with his knee.

CHAPTER 3

radle Bay High School looked like the kind of school Steve had seen on television. The main building was a tall, off-white structure that seemed to ooze respectability. A footpath led across a recently mowed lawn up to a short flight of clean steps. Three sets of doors were thrown wide open, allowing a stream of high-schoolers to surge into the corridors beyond.

Inside, the main hallway was wallpapered with homemade posters, flyers, and class announcements. EARN A BUCK—VOTE 4 CHUCK! SUPPORT YOUR SWIM TEAM—STATE CHAMPS 2 YEARS IN A ROW! And, most prominent of all, a huge banner running across the hallway read GO FORWARD! BE THE BEST—JOIN THE BLUE RIBBON CLUB!

Steve ducked under the sign and glanced at his school map. He found his first-period class, slipped inside, and dropped into a seat just as the bell rang.

English 12A—Advanced Placement English.

Focusing on the English novel from the 1800s to the present.

Not the best way to wake up in the morning, Steve thought.

Five minutes into class Steve had already pegged the teacher. Mr. Rooney was bald and personable. His vocabulary proved that he'd read every book on the list twice, and his speaking style gave you the impression that he might be a pushover—but probably wasn't.

With a wave of one long-fingered hand, Mr. Rooney invited a student to read a passage from the current novel: *Great Expectations* by Charles Dickens.

The boy who stood up was Trent Whalen. Steve pegged him almost as quickly as he'd pegged Mr. Rooney. Big. Blond. Letterman's jacket. Perfect teeth. Everything about him screamed dumb jock, except that he read like someone who had actually done the homework.

"'. . . and I had been so innocent and little there,'" Trent was reading, "'and all beyond was so unknown and great . . .'"

Mr. Rooney applauded. "Very good, Trent! To wit: When Pip says this, Dickens is speaking of the joy of discovery, of newness, of change." Rooney eyed Steve. "Mr. Clark, perhaps you can relate."

Steve sat up a little straighter. "Hmmm?"

"Hmmm," Mr. Rooney repeated, grinning at the class. "Mr. Clark is new to us from Chicago. Do they read Dickens in Chicago?"

"No, but we watch the movie version," Steve said with a laugh.

"Ah, the modern student's answer to homework! Just flip on the tube and soak it in through osmosis. No need to actually think! Now that's progress for you!"

Mr. Rooney was about to go on when the door flew open and a student stepped in wearing a torn leather jacket, motorcycle boots, and an oil-covered baseball cap. As he slouched across the front of the room, Steve saw the outline of a can of chewing tobacco in his back pocket.

Mr. Rooney leaned against his desk and sighed. "Well, well, if it isn't Dickie Atkinson. Say, weren't you in this class once upon a time? Tell us why you're late. Trouble with a camshaft?"

Dickie Atkinson dropped into a chair like a lead weight hitting bottom. "Like you know what one is."

Mr. Rooney thrust out his lower lip. "My, my, someone woke up on the wrong side of the carburetor this morning."

Atkinson shook his head and grumbled, "What a peckerhead."

Giggles rose from the class.

Rooney clutched his chest as if stabbed.

"*'Peckerhead!'*" he barked. "Once again, Mr. Atkinson reaches into his tiny Ziploc bag of insults and pulls out a true zinger. Although I confess I find myself stymied by your considerably arcane patois. What is—if I may be so forthright in displaying my ignorance—a 'peckerhead'?"

The class laughed again. They'd obviously seen Rooney put students in their place like this before.

Trent Whalen let out a loud chortle.

Atkinson glared at him. "What are you laughing at, Whalen?"

Trent smirked. "Nothing, nothing, Richard. I was just thinking that ignorance kills."

"What's that mean?"

"Exactly!" Trent said with another laugh.

"You butt-kissing little—" Atkinson jumped out of his seat and lunged for Whalen. He got his hands around Trent's throat and sent him tumbling backward out of his seat and to the floor. The two started grappling, but before either of them could get hurt, some of the other students jumped in, pulling them apart. Dickie Atkinson struggled against the hands that held him. Trent Whalen laughed as another jock in a Blue Ribbon jacket helped him to his feet.

Mr. Rooney stepped in, shaking his head.

"Perhaps, Mr. Atkinson, another trip to the principal would serve you well."

Atkinson shrugged off the students who held him and straightened his leather jacket. "You wanna know what a peckerhead is?" He jabbed a finger at Trent. "*That's* a peckerhead."

Mr. Rooney nodded. "Thank you for the clarification. Please send Principal Weathers our hosannas."

With a final scowl, Dickie Atkinson snatched up his fallen baseball cap and stormed from the room.

Steve glanced at Trent. Trent was looking at the friend who'd helped him off the floor. The two jocks exchanged a nod and a smile, then settled back into their seats.

By the time class was over, Steve wished *he'd* been sent to the principal's office. Mr. Rooney's snide remarks to the more troublesome students were the most interesting part of the class. His actual teaching was a yawnfest. When the bell rang, Steve slipped out with the crowd and walked across the campus to his next class. His route took him past the parking lot, just in time to see Dickie Atkinson jump into a 1969 Mustang Mach I. Atkinson peeled out of the lot, leaving a trail of burned rubber on the pavement.

"That's about the only mark that jerk's gonna leave on the world," said a voice beside Steve.

Steve turned to see the jock who'd helped Trent Whalen standing there.

"Hi," the guy said. "Robby Stewart."

"Steve Clark," Steve said. He nodded in the direction Dickie Atkinson had gone. "Looked like you and that guy Trent have it in for him."

Robby shrugged. "Just trying to help keep him in line."

Steve raised an eyebrow. "Is that your job?"

The other young man smiled. "What are friends for?"

Steve spent most of second period trying to figure out what Robby had meant by his strange comment and his confident smile. Steve noticed that a lot of students wore the Blue Ribbon logo on their shirts, and that they all had that same confident grin that Robby Stewart and Trent Whalen had flashed. Steve couldn't decide whether they were weird or he was still adjusting to a new school with a whole different lifestyle.

The lunch bell rang.

Steve walked into the cafeteria, not sure where to sit. He'd met a few people in his classes, but none of them had invited him to lunch. They had been polite enough, but at the same time, he could tell they'd been sizing him up, trying to put a label on him. It bugged him, but he tried to blow it off. If a new kid had arrived at his school

back in Chicago, he probably would have done
the same thing.

He chose an empty table and sat down to eat.

"These seats taken?"

He looked up to see a lean guy wearing
ragged jeans and an Anthrax T-shirt. Next to Mr.
Anthrax was the palest kid Steve had ever seen—
white skin, pale blue eyes, white hair. It took a
second for Steve to realize that he was an albino.

"No," Steve answered. "Go ahead."

The other two guys sat down. "I'm Gavin
Strick," the kid in the Anthrax T-shirt said.
"This here's Edward Vaugh, but everybody calls
him U.V."

"As in sunlight," U.V. said with a white-
toothed grin. "'Cause I get so much of it."

"I'm Steve."

Gavin nodded. "Yeah, I saw you in Mr.
Rooney's class this morning. You looked about as
bored as me, so I figured you couldn't be too
bad. Thought you could use some company for
lunch."

"So," U.V. said. "Give us the where from's and
why here's."

"Chicago," Steve answered. "And we moved
here because my parents just wanted to move."

"Out of the big city into the heartwarming
frontier lands?" Gavin asked. "Building good
character by mowing lawns, that sort of thing?"

"Yeah," Steve replied. "That's it."

Gavin snickered. "That's a boring story. There's gotta be something juicy in there you're not telling us."

"Nothing worth repeating," Steve said.

"Strick!"

A well-built man in his early forties, wearing shorts and a Cradle Bay High sweatshirt, strode up to their table. "Strick!" he repeated.

"Yes, Coach Bob!" Gavin called back with a mock salute.

"Strick, I wanna see you try out for the track team this year. Squirrelly guy like you could make it all the way to the sectionals!"

Gavin saluted again. "Thank you, Coach Bob, sir, but I would rather feast on the blistered skin of a half dozen A-bomb victims."

Coach Bob wasn't listening. "That's the spirit!" he said, already moving on to his next recruit.

Gavin shrugged at Steve. "What can you do, man? Some folks just don't get it."

Steve laughed.

"C'mon, U.V., let's eat." Gavin put a grocery store bag on the table and pulled out a huge, greasy hero sandwich. He then took out a green apple and passed it to U.V.

Steve did a double take at the size of the sandwich. "I see you're trying to stop world hunger by eating more."

Gavin grinned and took a wolf-sized bite. "Munchies. U.V. here has some primo weed. We burned a fatty during gym. Check him out—he looks almost tan, don't he?"

U.V. chomped away on his Granny Smith, nodding and smiling.

A girl in a clingy sweater passed their table. Gavin stopped eating midchew. Steve knew what he was looking at.

"Hey, Lorna!" Gavin said. "How are you today, my dear?"

Lorna looked at him and wrinkled her nose as if she'd just found maggots in her shrimp salad. "Drop dead, roach-head."

Gavin pumped his fist as if he'd just gotten her phone number. "Contact!"

"Who's that?" Steve asked, watching her walk away.

Gavin sighed and blew a kiss after her. "That, my boy, is Lorna "Love-itis" Longley. Fire of my loins. Purveyor of my every masturbatory fantasy. The entire female gender is separated into two groups, Stevie boy: Lorna Longley, and all the rest of 'em."

"You ever take her out?" Steve asked.

U.V. laughed, nearly choking on his apple. Gavin sighed like a man who'd just lost his heart. "Alas, Lorna is largely untouchable for someone of my social standing."

"What do you mean?" Steve asked.

Gavin nodded. "It's a class system here at C.B. High, Stevie boy. A shocking class system. Check it out."

He pointed at a pack of guys crowded around one table. They all looked like Dickie Atkinson clones. "There you got your motorheads. Car jocks. All the world's a gasket and a lube job and a pack of Luckys. Music of choice: posi-traction overdrive. Drug of choice: beer. Miller Genuine Draft. Keggers can't be choosers."

"Freaks who fix leaks," U.V. added.

"Now, over there," Gavin continued, pointing to a table where a few bookworms had gathered to eat peanut butter sandwiches, "you got your microgeeks. Nerds, whiz kids, and various other bottom feeders. If your books get dumped at least three times a day—chances are you're a microgeek. Music of choice: the sound of an Apple PC being booted up. Drug of choice: Stephen Hawking's *A Brief History of Time* and a cup of jasmine tea on a Saturday night."

"Freaks who squeak," U.V. put in.

Gavin continued his monologue, pointing his hero sandwich in the direction of some skateboarders in baggy pants and T-shirts. "There you got your skaters—rippin', ragin' dudes and their ramp tramps. Baggy pants, Dickies wools, doin' fifty-fifty Grinds with an Ollie Grab finish at a

homemade halfpipe in the woods. Music of
choice: the thwack of a Hacky Sack. Drug of
Choice: Ecstasy—longer loving through science."

"Freaks in sneaks!" U.V. piped up.

"So what about them?" Steve asked with a
laugh. He pointed at the table Lorna Longley
had chosen. Her table, and the three around it,
were filled with kids in Blue Ribbon jackets.
Steve recognized Trent Whalen and Robby
Stewart.

Gavin sucked air through his teeth. "Here's
where it gets really nasty. Call them jocks; call
them normals; call them the popular crowd.
They're Blue Ribbons—"

"What is that, anyway?" Steve asked.

"They're a community group," Gavin explained. "Good kids. Have bake sales and car
washes and kiss a lot of adult sphincter."

U.V. nodded. "Blue Ribbons equals Blue
Robots."

"Hear, hear," Gavin said, applauding. "See
those three guys next to Lorna? They're Cradle
Bay's answer to Eichmann, Himmler, and
Goebbels—"

"That's Nazis to the uneducated," U.V. said.

Gavin continued, "—Trent Whalen, Robby
Stewart, and Andy Effkin. Bet you didn't know
toast came in three flavors."

Steve zeroed in on a beautiful girl sitting at

the table in a designer outfit. "Speaking of flavors . . ."

"Oh, yes," Gavin growled. "That's Randi Sklar. Trent's woman, Lorna's best friend. Puts the *itch* in *bitch*. This group's music of choice: the hum of perfection, the buzz of ambition. Drug of choice: life. And the pursuit of clean living at the expense of all who sniffle at the hem of their gowns."

"Freaks so chic," U.V. concluded.

Steve shook his head. He couldn't help liking this squirrelly, fast-talking Gavin who'd plopped down at his table. "But that leaves you two—"

"Us?" Gavin said. "Kids like me and U.V., we're the leftovers. Lames who like their metal heavy and their Marlboros light. Music of choice—" Gavin and U.V. each twanged a metal riff. "Drug of choice: whattayagot?"

"Freaks all week!" U.V. hooted.

Gavin took a deep breath. "That's it. Lesson over. Class dismembered."

"Nice going." Steve smiled.

Gavin leaned over the table. "Welcome to Cradle Bay High, Stevie boy. Welcome to my nightmare."

CHAPTER 4

After a week Steve had started to settle into Cradle Bay. He still wasn't sure he'd made any real friends. He ate lunch with Gavin Strick, but Gavin's extracurricular activities generally revolved around lighting up some weed and raving about the system. Because Gavin was clever, his raves were better than most, but Steve got the impression that something was eating at Gavin that he didn't want to talk about.

As interesting as Gavin was, Steve wasn't sure they had that much in common. The crowd that most closely resembled Steve's old clique in Chicago was the Blue Ribbons . . . but this group just didn't feel the same. Back home (what *used* to be home, Steve reminded himself), they didn't have a club, or a slogan, or a Blue Ribbon logo. They were just a bunch of ordinary kids who enjoyed hanging out together. But here it was as if the "normals" had been made on an assembly line. They were all *exactly* the same. Same facial expressions, same gestures, same tone of voice, and all so peppy and upbeat, loving everything about school.

It was Wednesday night and all was well in the Clark household. The family had just finished dinner, and Lindsay and her new friend Shannon had pulled out a pile of flashcards and a dictionary and were sitting at the table testing their spelling while Mrs. Clark cleared the dishes. Steve and his father were at the other end of the table.

"Steve," Mr. Clark began gently, letting his elbows rest on the table, "I wanted to talk to you about how school's going."

"It's great," Steve said. "I got all the classes I wanted. I'm even ahead because of the work I was doing back in Chicago."

Mr. Clark scratched his forehead. "Not your classes, exactly. Your friends. I understand the only real friends you've made are . . . well . . . not exactly top of their class."

Steve raised an eyebrow. "Who told you what friends I've made?"

"People talk, Steve. Parents talk. And from what I've heard, this Strick boy is a drug user and a troublemaker. Not exactly your type."

Steve shrugged. "No one here's my type. The normals here are . . . they're not very *normal*."

Nathan Clark studied his son compassionately. "Steve, you should at least consider the fact that, after what happened back in Chicago, you might be trying to avoid all the things that remind you of . . . of that time. Some of it's best left in the past, but don't give up the good things." His father smiled. "I know you're smart enough to decide for yourself who to be friends with. But remember that first impressions are lasting impressions. If you want to fit in with the right group of people, you've got to help them feel comfortable around you right from the start."

"Phlegm!" Lindsay shouted suddenly.

"Phlegm," Shannon repeated. *"P-H-L-E-G-M-H."*

"Buzzzz!" Lindsay said, imitating a "wrong answer" alarm. "You added an extra *h* on the end."

"What are you girls doing?" Mrs. Clark asked.

Lindsay explained. "We're having a spelling bee against Hesel Junior High."

Shannon sighed and looked up the word in the dictionary. "And that was supposed to be an easy one. I don't get English. What's the big deal about sticking an extra *h* on the end, when there's a *g* in the middle that no one pronounces anyway?"

Lindsay shrugged. "My brother Allen could explain it to you. He was the best speller."

Shannon, all blond hair and blue eyes, looked up at Steve. "I thought your name was Steve."

"It is," he said.

"Steve's my other brother," Lindsay explained. "Allen's my brother who died."

"Oh," Shannon said. "I have a grandfather who died."

Mr. Clark sat back in his chair. "Why don't we change the subject?"

Steve felt tension cover the table like a cloud. It happened every time someone mentioned Allen—the same tension that had made them pick up and leave Chicago.

"Why?" Steve suddenly asked. "*Why* should we change the subject?"

Mr. Clark's brow was furrowed. "You know why."

Mrs. Clark spoke up. "It's okay, Nathan—"

"Tell me, Shannon," Steve said, interrupting. "Do you get yelled at if you talk about your dead grandfather?"

Steve's father leaned forward, his voice full of warning. "Steve—"

"—'cause around here, people go crazy if we talk about our dead brother!"

Before his father could react, Steve pushed his chair back from the dinner table and stormed out of the house.

The short walk into town helped Steve relax. He knew he shouldn't have blown up at his father. His parents and sister were trying to deal with his brother's death just as he was. But to Steve, dealing with it meant talking about it. To his parents, it seemed to mean locking bad memories away in some old house back in Chicago and moving to a new house where the memories couldn't find you.

Steve walked past the town square. In the middle lay a small park, and in the center of the park stood a statue of an angel with a small dog next to it. On the pedestal Steve noticed a small plaque that read SCOTTY BOSCO SQUARE: ONE HEARTACHE IS MORE THAN ENOUGH.

He left the park, passing by the brightly lit store with the words YOGURT SHOPPE painted in old-fashioned lettering on the wood sign overhead. Inside, the booths were packed with high-schoolers wearing letterman jackets with BLUE RIBBON stitched on the front and GO FORWARD below it.

Go forward, Steve thought. According to his parents, that was what they all had to do. *Go forward.*

He thought about what his father had said. These kids were the same sort he'd run with back home. So why wasn't he joining them now? Were they so different from his old friends? Or was *he* different now?

Robby Stewart looked up and saw Steve at the

window. He elbowed Trent Whalen, who also
looked. The two Blue Ribbons smiled and waved
Steve inside. He waved back, then hesitated.

Go forward, yeah, Steve thought. *But we've gotta
do it in our own time.*

He shrugged at Trent and Robby and pointed
at his watch, as if to say he was late somewhere.
Then he turned and walked away.

Behind him, Trent and Robby looked at each
other and frowned like two thieves who'd let a
prize slip through their fingers.

CHAPTER 5

The next day, as the final bell rang, the doors of Cradle Bay High School flew open and a flood of students rushed out like rats abandoning a sinking ship. Some students headed for their cars to go home or to after-school jobs; others swerved toward the gym for afternoon practice.

One clique of girls—all fashionably dressed, with well-coiffed hair and just the right amount of parent-approved makeup—headed straight for the Yogurt Shoppe. They all seemed to speak at the same time, in the kind of rushed whispers that meant they were gossiping. Every now and then the excitement got the better of them and their voices rose to a screech.

"No, no!" Randi Sklar shouted as they passed a hedge on the border of the school grounds. "I heard Mary Jo ran away with the cop . . . that he just up and left his wife and ran away with that tattooed fleabag."

"I heard Mexico!" said another.

"That is so Third World," Lorna Longley drawled. "Anyone who wants me to run away with them is taking me to Europe!"

Then their voices fell back to whispers and they moved on.

Behind the hedge, Gavin Strick and U.V. lay on their backs, staring up at the sky. Gavin passed his joint to U.V.

"You hear that?" the albino asked, toking on the joint.

"Yeah," Gavin said sullenly.

U.V. held in the hit for a minute, then let it out. "That's not what *you* said happened to Mary Jo and the cop."

Gavin snatched back his pot and inhaled deeply. "Yeah, well, who you gonna believe? Me or Randi Sklar?"

U.V. thought for a moment, then decided. "You, bud . . . definitely you. So what you gonna do about it?"

Gavin watched the smoke from his last toke rise into the sky, then immediately took another hit.

About a hundred yards away from Gavin and U.V., Steve sat in the office of Principal Weathers. Miss Perkins, the school guidance counselor, sat there with him. Beside Steve was an empty chair.

"Steven," Principal Weathers said, "we like to talk to all new students. Standard procedure. And as soon as Dr. Caldicott arrives, we can begin."

"Dr. Caldicott?" Steve asked.

Principal Weathers shook his head. "He's the resident faculty fellow. An outstanding educator. He's been with us for almost two years now. He works with the kids in a counseling capacity. I think you'll like him."

Miss Perkins leaned forward. "How are you finding your classes?"

With a map, Steve thought. Out loud he said, "Everything's fine."

Just then the door flew open and a man entered the office. He flashed a smile that managed to be friendly, apologetic, and self-confident all at once. He dropped lightly into the vacant chair.

"Sorry, folks. Sorry for being late." He shook Steve's hand. "Edgar Caldicott. Nice to finally meet you. How is everything?"

"Fine," Steve answered.

"Made any friends yet?" Caldicott asked.

Steve shrugged. "Yeah, I dunno. . . ." He decided that if Dr. Caldicott didn't already know he'd been hanging out with Gavin Strick, he wasn't going to tell him.

There was a brief silence, finally broken by Miss Perkins. "Have you given any thought to extracurricular activities? Sports?"

Steve thought about football, which he'd played back in Chicago. But then the picture of his brother in the muddy park came to mind, and he swallowed his response. "Not really."

Dr. Caldicott rubbed his hands together, and Steve had the distinct impression that he was about to roll up his sleeves in a serious "let's get cracking" way. "We have a number of exciting student groups involved in community service and social activities."

"Uh-huh," Steve said noncommitally.

"It's a great way to make friends," Miss Perkins added.

"And help your grade-point average," Principal Weathers said.

"It all comes down to what you're interested in, Steven," Dr. Caldicott concluded.

Steve felt his neck start to get sore from looking back and forth between the "educators."

Miss Perkins went on, "There's the Thespian Society, Politically Aware, Earth For Us. There's the Blue Ribbons—"

"Blue Ribbons," Steve said. "Who are they?"

Dr. Caldicott smiled. "They help each other study and practice. It's a team effort. A sort of motivational workshop, if you will. Blue Ribbon kids are truly making the grade and doing wonderful things on the playing field."

He looked at Steve, waiting for a response. Steve

had the feeling that Dr. Caldicott was waiting for him to say something in particular. But not knowing what it was, Steve said nothing.

"Steven," Principal Weathers said gently, "all of us here are aware of the tragedy back in Chicago, and we want you to know that—"

"I said everything's fine," Steve interrupted. He didn't know what they expected from him, but the last thing he wanted was their pity.

Dr. Caldicott nodded. "My family moved around quite a bit when I was your age. It's hard. Especially entering the middle of the school year. We know how tough it can be. So whether or not you want to be involved in the school, we want to be involved with you. We're here if you need us. That's all this meeting is about. Okay?"

Steve returned the doctor's steady gaze. When Caldicott had first entered the room, he'd reminded Steve of a talk show host—smooth and steady, confidently taking his emotional cues from a TelePrompTer. But now Steve had to admit that the man seemed genuinely concerned. Perhaps most importantly to Steve, he wasn't asking for anything. He hadn't asked Steve to spill his guts about his brother's death, and he wasn't asking for any sort of commitment to a club or group.

"Okay," Steve said. "Thanks."

Dr. Caldicott shook his hand again. "Good. Now go out and make some new friends."

Steve left the principal's office. In the main office, a kid in a Blue Ribbon jacket stitched with the name Andy Effkin happily sorted the teachers' mail into their boxes. In the hall, Steve passed the infirmary. A banner on the wall read BLOOD DRIVE TODAY! Some kids were lying down to donate blood, while others were being escorted from the couches by Blue Ribbon girls. The Blue Ribbons had juice and cookies ready and waiting. Everyone had been persuaded to donate, and Steve had done so earlier in the day.

As Steve passed the blood drive, he caught the eye of Lorna Longley. He smiled, and she smiled back, holding his gaze for an extra second before turning away.

If Lorna Longley was the girl next door, five minutes later Steve met the girl from the wrong side of the tracks.

Leaving the main school building, he walked through the parking lot toward the growing sound of rock music blaring from a battered pickup truck. In the bed of the truck he saw the girl his mother had always warned him about dancing in torn jeans and a baggy sweater. She wore dark makeup, had several tattoos, and wore a silver ring in her nose that matched the one in her navel. Her long, dark hair fell over her shoulders, and she was dancing like a pro. Steve immediately knew this girl was everything Lorna Longley was not. Which meant, he realized, that she had character.

"You like that, do you?"

Gavin Strick had materialized next to him. He wore a T-shirt with the slogan SICK OF IT ALL.

"Who is it?" Steve asked.

Gavin threw an arm around Steve's shoulder. "My buddy, Rachel. Cook's Ridge trash. From the wrong side of the track—the bad part of town. Great chick, don't get me wrong. But Cook's Ridge trash."

Steve raised an eyebrow. "If that's trash, get me a job at the sanitation department."

"A joke!" Gavin said, stepping back and applauding. "What do you know? Come on." He led Steve over to the truck and, more importantly, to the girl. "Rachel, this is Stevie boy. Good man. Stevie boy, this is Rachel. Cook's Ridge trash."

Rachel glared at Gavin. "Bite me." Then, to Steve, she said, "Hey."

"Hey," he said back.

Eye contact. Steve noticed Rachel sizing him up, but he didn't mind. He could have stared at her all afternoon.

"Woo-hoo!" Gavin called. "Appropriate sparks are flying. Somebody cue the power ballad!"

Rachel brushed a stray lock of hair behind an ear. "Fail to be a tumor, Gavin."

Gavin shrugged and lit two cigarettes, handing one to Rachel. "Say," he suggested, "what do you say we cruise town, chase a case, hit the shore, and drink some beer. Consecrate Stevie boy's arrival to this pathetic tank town. You down?"

Rachel hadn't stopped looking at Steve. "Sounds razor."

"Stevie boy?" Gavin asked.

Steve smiled at Rachel. "Sure."

They climbed into Rachel's pickup truck. "So," Steve asked, looking for something to say. "Can this heap get anywhere?"

"It'll do," Rachel said. She gunned the engine and dropped into gear. The truck shot forward, Steve's head snapped back, and for the rest of the trip he held on for dear life.

CHAPTER 6

There was an art, Gavin explained on the way to the Cradle Bay Supermarket, to getting adults to buy liquor for minors. You had to pick the right adult, say the right words, and have the right look.

If that was true, then by about nine P.M. Gavin had struck out on all three counts—several times over. Steve and Rachel sat in the back of her pickup truck in the parking lot as Gavin returned from another failed attempt.

"The problem with America as we lurch ever so close to the dawn of the twenty-first century," he said, "is mankind's abject unwillingness to contribute to the delinquency of minors."

"We don't need the beer," Steve said. "Why not just hang out?"

"Whoa, boy," Gavin said. "That's Blue Ribbon talk there. Them's fightin' words."

Steve raised an eyebrow. "What do you mean?"

Gavin jumped into the back of the truck and lay down, staring up at the night sky. Even through the bright lights of the nearby market, a crowd of stars was visible. "Get with the program, Stevie, my friend. You've been here long enough to notice that the school is divided into two groups. Blue Ribbons, and the kids who're still willing to be kids. Namely, do stupid things, play stupid pranks, drink beer even though we're underage. Fun stuff."

Steve shrugged. "So you're saying that if I decide not to drink a beer, I'm a Blue Ribbon?"

"Could be," Gavin said, a mischievous gleam in his eye. "Rachel, let's check for pods. He may have been body-snatched."

Rachel had a gleam in her eye too, but of a different nature. "I'll do the checking."

Steve laughed. "Don't get me wrong, I never claimed to be perfect. I'm just saying that if you do stuff just to prove you're not like them, you're not doing it because you want to."

"Best of both worlds, Stevie boy," Gavin insisted. "Kill two birds with one stone. Question authority and get a buzz at the same time. Now, that is what adolescence is all about!"

At the sound of approaching footsteps, he popped upright. "And speaking of adolescence . . ."

Steve followed his gaze. A big, beefy teenager

with a crew cut, wearing a football jersey, lumbered toward them. His thick neck had almost vanished beneath the huge muscles of his shoulders. His forward slope reminded Steve of the scoop on a bulldozer.

"Hello, Rachel," the guy said with a smile.

"Hey, Chug," she replied.

Chug glanced at Steve and Gavin. "What are you doing?" he asked Rachel.

"Chasing a case," she said. "Nobody's buying."

"So, Charles," Gavin said with a yawn. "Cycle any good anabolic steroids lately?"

"Very funny, Strick," Chug said.

Gavin bowed. "Thank you, thank you. Here all week. Come see the show again."

Chug's eyes flicked back to Rachel. Then they flicked up and down, admiring her. "Some of us'll be at the Yogurt Shoppe later on, if you wanna—"

"The Yogurt Shoppy!" Gavin broke in. "Yogurt—the dessert for those with culture!"

Chug looked at Gavin as if he was a mosquito he'd like to slap dead. "See ya, Rachel."

"Bye." Rachel flashed a smile his way.

Steve suddenly felt jealous.

"I don't believe you," Gavin said to Rachel when Chug was gone. "You are actually flattered that barn door has a thing for you."

"Get bent," she said, with a glance at Steve.

When she saw the jealous look in his eye, she smiled.

Chug Roman slouched through the supermarket's automatic doors with Rachel still on his mind. The refrigerated air inside the market made him feel better, but not great. His skin felt too warm, as if he was wearing all his pads, his uniform, and his football helmet. Seeing Rachel had made him hot, and that made him irritable.

He stalked down the aisle, a hunter-gatherer looking for a meal, until he reached the dairy section. He snatched up a carton of protein drink, then headed for the cash register.

There were two skateboarders ahead of him in line.

"So we were just pulling Ollies off the front steps an' this security dude jumps outta nowhere and starts raggin' on us," one of them said to the other.

"Bogus," said the other.

Punks, Chug thought. *Hurry up, punks.*

Beyond the cash register, through the store's front window, he could see Rachel still talking with Gavin and the new kid. She laughed at something the new kid had said and brushed back her hair. Chug liked it when she did that.

"Hey, I gotta joke for you," the second skate rat said. He pulled open a carton of milk.

Chug noticed that there was a space in front of the skateboarder where he could step forward. *The punk should move up in line,* Chug thought.

He glanced out the window. Rachel was holding her hands over her head. Her crop top rode up, revealing the ring in her navel. Chug felt sweat trickle down his forehead.

"What did the hooker say after twelve hours on the job?" the skate rat asked.

Move forward in line, idiot-punk, Chug thought.

"What?" asked the skate rat's buddy.

The skateboarder took a huge swig of milk and let it dribble down his chin as he answered, "God, I'm tired."

"Dude, that's nasty!" his partner said, chortling.

Chug stared at Rachel, feeling a twitch in his eye, where a tiny wedge-shaped chip flashed briefly. He could see Rachel, her hair, her face, her eyes. Her body. "Go forward," he muttered.

"Huh?" the skateboarders asked, looking around. "What up?"

Chug clenched his fists, forgetting he was holding the carton of protein drink. The carton exploded, sending up a shower of pink liquid. The two skateboarders stepped back, but they were too slow. Chug grabbed one in either hand, lifting them as if they were rag dolls and slamming them onto the floor.

CHAPTER 7

"Get off me, du—" one of the skateboarders yelled, but his cry was cut off as Chug picked him up and threw him into one of the aisles. Cans and boxes went flying.

The other skate rat tried to crawl away. Chug stepped on his back, forcing him flat, then slammed his other foot on the boy's head. His hands and feet pounded to the same rhythm as he wailed on the two punks, beating them all over their bodies.

The pounding in his head stopped. Chug felt hands on him, realized he was being held down. He blinked and looked up into the face of Officer Cox.

Beyond Officer Cox, one of the skateboarders had crawled to his feet. His face was a bloody mess. "What's up with you, man? Goddamn Blue Ribbon bastard!"

The pounding returned with a roar. Chug let it

take him over and went with it. He threw Officer Cox off him and leaped to his feet. He charged, grabbing the skateboarder like a tackling dummy and driving him toward the meat counter.

"Noooo!" the punk screamed.

Chug crushed the skateboarder's bloody face between a pastrami and a brisket.

Steve, Gavin, and Rachel had heard the shouting and entered the store along with a crowd of onlookers. Stunned, they watched Officer Cox pull Chug off his victim and drag him aside. Instantly Chug became calm. He blinked and looked around as if wondering who was responsible for all the commotion.

"What was that all about?" Steve asked.

"Toxic Jock Syndrome," Rachel guessed.

Gavin stared, shocked, remembering Andy Effkin at the Bluffs.

Officer Cox waved the crowd back. "Okay, people. Calm down. Everything's all right."

Gavin's face went deathly pale and he turned away, hurrying back toward the pickup.

He didn't say a word about it.

With nowhere special to go and no suggestions, Rachel drove them out to the shore. Before she had even shifted the truck into park, Gavin jumped out and was heading toward the beach.

"What the hell would make a kid freak like that?" Steve asked.

"It's gotta be a steroid thing," Rachel guessed. "All those jockos are into it. Kelly Connor said she saw Andy Effkin bite the head off a kitten in a fit of rage."

"Oh, yeah, that always helps me calm down," Steve said.

"Serious. I think it's bull, though."

Gavin turned and glared at them both. "It's not bull. And it's not steroids."

Rachel rolled her eyes. "Here we go."

"What?" Steve asked.

"Gavin thinks there's some sinister force taking over the Cradle Bay meatheads."

Steve blinked. "Some sinister force?"

Rachel winked. "You know: evil. Bad mojo. The total wiggins. Nowhere to turn. No one to trust. Altogether ooky."

Gavin looked as if he wanted to protest, but instead he just stuck his hands in his pockets. "Fail to be a bitch, Rachel."

"Fail to be a pucker-ass, Gav!" she replied. She blew him a kiss.

Gavin snatched the imaginary kiss out of the air, threw it down, and squashed it like a bug. Then he turned and took off down the beach, disappearing into the dark.

Steve watched him go, then looked at Rachel. "You know what he's talking about?"

She shook her head. "He's kind of short in the detail department. And look, I love Gav, he's a trip, but he also tokes on a regular basis." She held two fingers to her mouth and puffed. "That doesn't make for unbiased reporting."

Steve looked back into the darkness. Rachel had a point. But he couldn't help thinking that for a guy who joked about everything else, Gavin was awfully serious about this.

CHAPTER 8

If there was an undesirable part of Cradle Bay, its center lay at the corner of Michael Street and Vincent, where Dickie Atkinson lived with his mom on the ground floor of a duplex. Dickie was draped across the worn-out couch, watching TV with the volume up loud. The cable was working again, so he'd turned up ESPN's *RPM Tonight*. Stock-car racing.

Now if only I had some brew, he thought.

The neighbors upstairs complained about the noise by stomping on the ceiling. Dickie responded by turning up the TV so that he couldn't hear the stomping.

Over the din, the phone rang. Delores Atkinson hurried from the kitchen, holding a pile of mail she'd been sorting.

"Hello?" she said, trying to plug her ear. She could barely make out the voice on the other end. She listened for a moment, then nodded. "Dickie, it's for you!"

"Who is it?" he shouted.

"Someone about your car!"

Instantly Dickie hit the Mute button on the remote, and the sounds of revving engines and sportscasters went silent. Dickie vaulted over the couch and snatched the phone from his mother's hand.

"Yo," he said.

A dry, husky voice replied, "You called me about car parts?"

"Yeah," Dickie said. "I was calling about the rear louvers."

He noticed his mom still hovering nearby and scowled at her.

The man on the other end started to cough as if he was hacking up a lung. "Sorry. Been trying to quit the cigarettes."

"Yeah, well, listen—" Dickie glared at his mom, covered the mouthpiece, grabbed the pile of mail she'd been flipping through, and heaved it across the room, where it scattered into a chaotic mess. "Read that crap over there!"

Delores Atkinson stood, her eyes welling with tears.

"You still there?" the smoker's voice asked.

"Yeah, yeah." Dickie glared at his mother. *"Go away,"* he ordered.

"What model you got?" the man rasped.

"A sixty-nine Mustang Mach One," Dickie answered.

The smoker on the other end laughed. "Yeah, I got just what you need. Cost you two-fifty. But I'm leavin' pretty soon. Can you come by now?"

"What's the address?" Dickie wrote it on a slip of paper, slammed down the phone, and strode past his mother.

Delores Atkinson bent down to gather the mail off the floor. As she heard the back door slam, she fell to her knees and burst into tears.

The address the old man had given Dickie led to the dark outskirts of Cradle Bay. Nothing new to Dickie. Most motorheads did their work in the industrial parts of town, away from the main streets where wise-ass neighbors complained about engine noise and oil stains.

The place turned out to be a trailer near an abandoned-looking shipyard wharf. Dickie parked his Mustang and got out, double-checking the address in the distant light of the only streetlamp for half a mile.

"What a goddamn dump," he said. It looked as if nobody had lived in the trailer for years.

Someone coughed behind him. Dickie whirled. There was nothing but darkness.

"Hello?" he called out.

Click. A flashlight beam appeared, shining right into his face. Then another, and another, all blinding him. He was surrounded by lights.

"What the—" he started to say.

One of the flashlights was suddenly aimed under the chin of the person holding it. Blinking, Dickie saw the face of Trent Whalen lit by the weird glow.

More figures stepped into the dim light. Dickie didn't know their names, but he recognized the BLUE RIBBON on the boys' jackets. Then more appeared. He saw Robby Stewart step forward. The guys all held baseball bats and large sticks.

"What are you guys doing here?" Atkinson asked.

The group slowly closed in on him.

Robby coughed like an old man and rasped, "Sorry. Been trying to quit the cigarettes."

Andy Effkin stepped toward Dickie. "The troops shall set you free. . . ."

Dickie was surrounded. "What do you want?"

"You, sweet Dickie," Trent answered. "We want you."

"Yeah," Robby agreed. "We've got it for you, Richard. We've got your hubcap diamond-star halo."

They swarmed over Dickie, bats and sticks raised.

* * *

Dickie woke with a start. It was dark, just as it had been in the shipyard. His face felt a little puffy, where he guessed they'd hit him, but otherwise he didn't seem to be hurt. He remembered the bastard Blue Ribbon freaks crowding in around him, but he didn't remember much after that. Still, he couldn't be beaten up too badly. Had they decided to leave him alone?

Their mistake, he thought. He'd get a few of the guys from auto shop together, borrow a couple of tire irons, and teach those do-goody wussies to gang up on—

Dickie tried to move his hands but couldn't. They were tied down, as were his feet. He tried to tilt his chin, but his head was tied down too.

"What's going on?" he asked. "Hey, what's going on here?"

As if on cue, a single thin beam of light appeared, shooting straight into Dickie Atkinson's right eye. A moment later he heard the shrill whine of a drill bit. The light drew nearer and the drill's whine grew louder. It seemed to be heading right for his eye. They were going to stick it in his eye.

Dickie Atkinson let out a bloodcurdling scream.

CHAPTER 9

When Steve Clark learned that his social studies class was going on a field trip, he assumed they'd end up at a natural history museum or the local American Legion hall. So he was mildly surprised when he, Gavin, and a busload of other high-schoolers ended up at Cradle Bay Hospital.

He was even more surprised when, instead of taking the elevators up to one of the hospital wards, they went down to the basement.

Miss Perkins, acting as chaperone, led them through a pair of swinging doors marked MORGUE. Beyond the doors lay a figure covered by a sheet. Beside it stood a man dressed in a hospital smock and mask—the coroner. The room was cold enough to make Steve shiver.

Once all the students had gathered, Miss Perkins nodded to the coroner, who threw back the sheet. Half the students squealed in disgust; the rest choked.

Beneath the sheet lay the corpse of a man, the skin light blue and covered with bruises. His neck was twisted at an awkward angle, and the left side of his head had been bashed in by some blunt object. Brains and blood, now drying, were splattered over what remained of his face.

A couple of students gagged and ran out of the room.

"Mr. Gray here," the coroner explained dryly, "had a blood alcohol level three times the legal limit when his car ran into a telephone pole."

Steve leaned back, trying to keep his distance from the corpse. He saw Trent Whalen and Robby Stewart lean forward. Beside him, Gavin gagged and pushed his way out of the room, holding one hand over his mouth.

Miss Perkins addressed the class. "Since Scotty Bosco's death, drunk driving incidents have decreased by over sixty percent in Cradle Bay. That's good news. But until we've eliminated the threat entirely, we'll continue to show you students the tragic consequences of drinking and driving."

Outside, Gavin hurried down the hall. Miss Perkins's voice grew distant.

Gavin pulled out his lighter and a cigarette. When he heard footsteps approaching from around a corner, he ducked through the nearest door, which was marked MORGUE STORAGE ROOM. The dark room was full of shelves lined with jars. Gavin glanced at the closest one and shuddered. Floating in amber-colored fluid was a blackened lung. He looked down at his cigarette, then shrugged. "Nice."

He started to light up, but then he heard voices heading in his direction.

"Jeez, you'd think a guy'd find some peace and quiet in the *morgue*," he muttered. He moved to the far end of the storage room and found a door marked REFRIGERATOR. When he pulled the handle, the door opened with a soft click and he slipped inside.

The room was freezing, but he didn't care. He lit up the cigarette and took a long drag, leaning against the table in the room's center. He felt something brush his arm and looked down to see a big white toe rubbing against his skin.

"Goddamn!" he shouted, choking on his cigarette. Lying on the table was the corpse of a fat man, totally naked.

Beneath the body, on a second shelf, lay another. This body was covered with a sheet from head to ankle, with only the feet exposed. By the red toenails, looking gruesome against the dead white flesh, Gavin guessed it was female. He was about to turn away when something else caught his eye.

A tattoo.

On the corpse's ankle was a tattoo of the devil and the initials *M.J.C.*

Mary Jo Copeland.

CHAPTER 10

Mary Jo Copeland's corpse. Here, in the Cradle Bay morgue, not on a rendezvous in Mexico getting a tan. Why hadn't anyone said so? Why had everyone said she'd run away?

Gavin reached out for the tag tied to one of the toes and lifted it with the tips of his fingers. The tag read simply JANE DOE.

Trembling, Gavin moved to the head of the table. He had started to lift the sheet to see her face when the door of the refrigeration room opened. Miss Perkins stood framed in the doorway.

"Gavin Strick!"

He felt his heart leap into his throat as he jumped away from the table.

"What are you doing in here?" Miss Perkins demanded. She sniffed the air, then glanced at the cigarette still burning in Gavin's hands. "And you're smoking? Put that out and get back into the other room. You're getting written up for this, young man!"

Gavin glanced back at the shape under the sheet and calmly walked past Miss Perkins. Inside, he felt as if his bones had turned to jelly. Mary Jo Copeland was here. And someone knew it. But nobody was telling.

"So how can you be sure it was her?" Steve asked.

He and Gavin were walking down a flight of stairs to the basement of Cradle Bay High School. Gavin had made like a clam during the bus ride home, but he'd insisted Steve meet up with him after the final bell rang. They'd met outside, and Gavin had told Steve what he'd seen at the Bluffs between Mary Jo and Andy Effkin. Now Steve and Gavin were stomping down to the bowels of the building.

"I knew her, Stevie boy," Gavin insisted. "Besides, in a town the size of Cradle Bay, how many girls you figure have a tattoo of the devil with *M.J.C.* underneath?"

At the bottom of the steps, Gavin opened the door of the boiler room. Two big, black boilers clanked and chugged, giving off a feeble glow. A third was silent. The room was sooty and dark, like the inside of an oven when the light has burned out.

"So what are we doing down here?" Steve asked.

"This is Cancer Corner," Gavin said, sitting down on an empty crate. "Best place in the school to sneak a smoke." He stopped at the silent furnace and reached inside, pulling out a stash of cigarettes.

"They say she ran away," he said. "But I saw her get killed. Now I can prove it."

Steve studied his friend. "Look, Gav, it's not like I don't want to believe you. But why didn't you go to the police?"

Gavin threw down his cigarette. "The police were there, man, and that cop didn't do jack."

"Hey!"

A face appeared behind them, scowling. Steve and Gavin jumped. In the faint light of the furnaces, they could see that the newcomer's face was angular and pockmarked.

Steve backed away, but Gavin settled back down to light up another smoke. "Hey, Dorian, what's up?"

"Who—?" Steve started to ask.

Gavin nodded at the scar-faced man, who was still scowling at them. "That's Mr. Dorian Newberry, janitor extraordinaire."

"Custodian," Newberry corrected. "As in *caretaker*. From the Latin *custodia*. As in *watchman*."

"Mr. Newberry," Gavin observed, "takes his job very seriously."

"What are you turds doing here?" the custodian demanded. "You ain't supposed to be down here."

"I was just showing my friend Stevie around. Steve's new to the Bay—"

"New to the Bay?" Newberry snorted, as though it couldn't be true. His eyes took on a very unnatural light. "Hmmm. New to the Bay. Gnaw, gnaw, gnaw! *Rattus rattus!* Aha! Excreta! And drag marks . . . the drag marks of rat tails!"

"Um," Steve said, flabbergasted. "Okay."

Gavin didn't seem thrown by Newberry's odd outburst. He just pointed one finger at his own head and twirled it around. Then he pointed to a box in the custodian's hand. "What do you have there, Mr. Newberry?"

Newberry held up the black box. One side was painted with the word IR-RAT-ICATOR. "Sounds're supposed to scare the rats away," he explained.

He twisted a knob on the side of the black box and the device began to emit a weak, high-pitched squeak.

Newberry eyed them both. "You hear that?"

"Yeah," Steve said.

"Scary, huh?" Newberry said sarcastically. He tossed the Ir-rat-icator aside. "Damn things don't work worth spit." He picked up the black box and started tinkering with it.

Gavin answered Steve's unanswered question. "Yeah, he's nuts. Mr. Newberry's got that whole village idiot, Boo Radley, Quasimodo thing going, don't you, Mr. Newberry?"

"Hmmph," Newberry grunted.

Gavin jabbed his cigarette in the direction of the black box. "He's currently engaged in a war against the rodent population of Cradle Bay."

A sudden squeak filled the air, but it wasn't coming from the black box. It was coming from the corner, where a thick-tailed rat scampered toward a hole in the wall. Quicker than lightning, Newberry snatched up a hammer and dashed after the rodent, yelling, "Got to fight 'em. Gotta fight. Rats from the Bay. *Rattus rattus.* The carrier of the plague. Black death. Forty rats are born in America every second. That's a lotta plague!"

Cackling, the custodian moved off into the darkness.

Steve had to tear his attention from the bizarre man, who was banging away in the dark corners. "So listen, Gavin, if you're really sure about this, you've got to tell someone. The principal or the newspapers or—"

"Now, why didn't I think of that!" Gavin said, smacking himself on the side of the head. Then he added sarcastically, "No, wait a minute. I did think of that. But then I remembered that I'm just a punk kid who inhales reefer all day and listens to too much suicidal heavy metal, and that I'd be telling people that a respected police officer and the star quarterback are liars and murderers *and I figured I'd think twice about doing that!*" Gavin whirled and ran for the stairs.

Steve took off behind him, trying to catch up. He was no psychologist, but he could tell Gavin was being eaten up by what he'd seen, and the fact that he didn't know whom to tell. And he had to admit, Gavin did have a point. Who would have believed him?

Steve didn't catch up to Gavin until they were outside on the school grounds.

"Look, Gavin, I'm sorry," he said. "I'm just trying to—"

But he realized his friend wasn't listening. Gavin was staring out into the parking lot, where a crowd of students had gathered around a 1969 Mustang Mach I. Over the car hung a banner that read SLEDGE FEST: TWO WHACKS FOR $1.00.

Steve joined the small crowd, stepping up next to Gavin, Rachel, and U.V. He recognized the car as the one Dickie Atkinson had been driving his first day at school.

Next to the car, Trent Whalen handed a sledgehammer to Lorna Longley. Using all her strength, and managing to look pretty at the

same time, Lorna lifted the sledgehammer and
let loose. Her blow shattered one of the headlights, and she let out a sadistic laugh.

"Beautiful, huh," U.V. said sarcastically.

Gavin shook his head. "Welcome to a Day at
the Master Races."

"Check that out," Rachel said. "Look."

Lorna handed the sledgehammer to the next
kid in line. The kid wore wide-wale corduroy
pants, a Stanford University sweatshirt, and brand-
new Reeboks. He looked like the poster boy for a
software company. But beneath the prep-school
primping was a face they all recognized.

The face of Dickie Atkinson.

CHAPTER 11

Dickie Atkinson raised the sledgehammer and let out a loud hoot as he brought it crashing down on the windshield.

"Dickie?" Gavin called out, shaken by the change in him.

Atkinson didn't answer. He raised the sledge-hammer and bashed in the driver's side door.

U.V. shook his head. "He's one of them now. A Blue Robot."

Gavin looked around and spotted a small group of motorheads sitting on and around a primer-gray Chevy Camaro. They watched in utter disbelief as Dickie Atkinson gleefully trashed the car he'd spent his entire high-school career rebuilding.

"Look at 'em," Gavin rasped. "The apes. They have no idea why Dickie's suddenly hangin' with the jocks and jerks."

"Why is he?" Steve asked.

"Yeah, he hates those creeps," Rachel added.

"Maybe he turned over a new leaf," U.V. suggested.

Gavin snorted. "I'd like to own the new-leaf concession here in Cradle Bay."

U.V. nodded at Steve. "Gavin, you tell him about the body?"

Gavin shrugged. "Stevie boy's a disbeliever."

Steve took a deep breath. "Look, Gav, all I'm saying is that you admitted you were high that night. And even if Andy Effkin was some kind of killer, why would Officer Cox hide it when his own partner had been killed?"

Gavin shrugged. "I'm not saying I know the whole story. But I know what I saw." He looked from one face to another, recognizing the doubt in their eyes. "So we're back on this page. This is where you accuse me of being paranoid."

"Denial ain't just a river in Italy, " U.V. joked incorrectly.

"Check your weed, Gav," Steve said. "That's all."

Gavin glared at Steve. "You are beige, boy—"

Steve shot him a look. He told himself that Gavin was a punk and a pothead and a slacker. "I'm outta here," he said.

Steve Clark had had enough of Gavin Strick. He'd had enough of hanging with the outcasts who'd decided he was cool because he'd been rejected by the popular crowd. Steve probably wouldn't have made friends with Gavin in the first place if Gavin hadn't known Rachel. And now that Steve knew Rachel himself, she'd either like him or she wouldn't. That was up to her, and Steve didn't need Gavin for that.

Steve headed into the Yogurt Shoppe.

The place was packed with Blue Ribbons. All eyes turned to him. Momentarily his steps faltered, but he pulled himself together, walked up to the counter, and ordered. Trent Whalen slid up beside him and slapped him on the back.

"Steven! Good to see you, brother!"

Steve smiled. "Hey, Trent." The server handed him a cup full of chocolate-vanilla swirl.

"Come sit down," Trent invited him.

Trent led Steve to a booth filled with the big names on Cradle Bay's campus: Andy Effkin, Robby Stewart, Chug Roman (who had bruises on his face from his fight at the market the other night), Lorna Longley, Randi Sklar, and Dickie Atkinson. Several of them scooted over to make room for him.

"Hey, guys," Trent said, "this is Steven. He's new to the Bay. From Chicago."

"Do you like it here?" Randi asked him, beaming.

"It's all right," Steve answered.

Dickie Atkinson nodded in agreement. "You had friends in Chicago?"

"Yeah."

Lorna Longley leaned forward and dipped her spoon into Steve's yogurt. "You can have friends here."

Steve caught the inviting look in her eye and returned it, until another sort of curiosity got the best of him. He looked at Trent and Dickie Atkinson. "Didn't you guys get into a fight in English?"

Trent waved that off. "We've made peace, Steven. It's what separates us from the animals."

Lorna stiffened. "Uh-oh. Dirtbag alert." She waved a hand.

Steve followed her gesture to the door of the Yogurt Shoppe, where Gavin Strick stood. He glanced around until his eyes settled on Steve. Just a hint of betrayal showed in his expression before he covered it with his usual sarcastic grin. "Stevie boy! I gotta talk to you."

Trent stood. "Easy, Slick. Steven's relaxing."

Gavin didn't believe it. "Just look at this place. The Yogurt Shoppe? Or is it pronounced Yogurt Shoppy? What the hell is a shoppy anyway? What's the *e* on the end for?"

Randi Sklar glared daggers at Gavin. "Why, Gavin Strick, can't you make like a tree and leave?"

"Ooh, clever girl," he replied. He leaned over Steve. "What are you doing here?" he whispered. "We get into one argument and you go bond with the bad guys?"

Chug Roman stood and glowered at Gavin. Gavin smiled at the big Blue Ribbon's bruises. "What happened to you, Charles? Too much flank steak?"

Chug took a step forward. Gavin held his ground. Before the situation could escalate, Steve slipped between them. He still didn't know what to think of any of the kids in Cradle Bay, but at least he'd narrowed down the mystery to this: Despite Gavin's weirdly paranoid behavior, he liked him, and despite the Blue Ribbons' weirdly normal behavior, he disliked them.

"Let's go," he said to Gavin.

Trent put a hand on Steve's shoulder. "You don't have to go anywhere, brother."

Gently but firmly, Steve removed the other boy's hand. "I'm not your brother."

Steve followed Gavin out the door, feeling the eyes of the Blue Ribbons burrowing into his back.

The two teens walked across the town square until the Yogurt Shoppe was out of sight. "Okay," Steve said. "I'm here. What?"

Gavin gathered himself, then said, "They're hypnotized."

Steve blinked. He'd been expecting something else—maybe some sort of apology for Gavin's behavior, maybe a story about an alcoholic father or a negligent mother who filled Gavin with a need to smoke pot and make up stories to make life seem more interesting and less unhappy. This, however, Steve couldn't follow. "Huh?" he asked.

Gavin tried again. "Okay. Maybe not hypnotized. Brainwashed. Lobotomized. Programmed. You want proof? Here's proof."

He pulled a photograph from his jacket pocket and handed it to Steve. At first Steve didn't see what he was getting at. It was a picture of Gavin with two guys and a girl. They were gathered around a huge bong, partying hard. The kids were wearing denim jackets, torn jeans, and rock concert T-shirts. Steve didn't get why Gavin was showing him this. Then he noticed the girl's face.

The girl was Randi Sklar, and the boys—the boys were Trent Whalen and Robby Stewart. But they all looked completely different from the kids Steve had met at the Yogurt Shoppe. In the picture, they didn't look much younger than they were now. They must have gone through a radical change pretty recently. Still, that didn't prove anything.

Steve handed the picture back. "Maybe they just got sick of your rap. I can relate."

Gavin set his jaw. "I figured you'd say that. That's the purpose of tonight's excursion. After tonight, you'll be paying a great deal more attention to my rap. Come along. I have something to show you."

CHAPTER 12

High-school campuses at night gave Steve the creeps. All day long they were bright, noisy, and full of life. Bells screeched the hour, feet tramped through the hallways.

But at night it all stopped, became frozen and tense, as if the whole place was holding its breath, waiting for something to happen.

Gavin led Steve toward the main building.

"You sure we can get in here?" Steve asked.

Gavin laughed. "You kidding? No one in Cradle Bay locks their front door. You think they'd lock up the school?"

The two boys hurried around to the side of the building, where a basement window sat close to the ground. Gavin popped it open with ease, and they slipped inside.

They were in the boiler room, moving through the dim light cast by the chugging furnaces.

"Now what?" Steve asked.

Gavin tiptoed over to a ventilator shaft. A maintenance ladder led up to the metal grille covering the shaft. Gavin climbed it, yanked the grille away, and handed it to Steve, who set it gently on the ground. Gavin peered into the ventilator shaft and motioned for Steve to come up. Steve hesitated, then followed.

Gavin leaned into the shaft, then yelled, "Yuck!" and lurched back, staring at his hand. He waved it, shaking something away. It fell past Steve.

"Excreta!" Gavin said, gagging.

Steve flinched. "*What!* Where are we going?" he whispered.

"Shhh!" Gavin replied. "Voices carry. Down here things can echo." He disappeared into the shaft. Wiping his forehead, Steve followed.

Neither one of them noticed the figure lurking in the shadows beside the furnaces.

The ventilator shaft was wide enough to let them crawl on their hands and knees. There were enough turns and branching tunnels to get them hopelessly lost, but Gavin seemed to know exactly where he was going. Their trip ended at a metal grille like the one they'd used to enter the vent system. This one opened out into the auditorium.

At Gavin's signal, Steve crawled up beside him until they were both pressed against the grille, looking down on the auditorium.

"Blue Ribbon meeting," Gavin whispered. "Every Monday. This is where it all goes down."

There were about thirty parents in attendance. On the stage sat Principal Weathers, Miss Perkins, and Dr. Caldicott, who seemed to be running the meeting. He waited patiently as Miss Perkins finished reading a report.

". . . and by conducting the bake sale in conjunction with the pep rally, we can be selling cakes and cookies at a time when school spirit is at its optimum level."

Steve stared wide-eyed at Gavin. "I had no idea evil was this pervasive," he said sarcastically.

"Just listen." Gavin was deadly serious.

A man stood up in the audience. "I just wanted to say that before we sent our son to Dr. Caldicott, we were . . . well, we were living under siege. Our boy was wild, reckless, drinking, drugging. . . . Now his grades have skyrocketed, he's gone out for the wrestling team. And I actually cannot wait to get home from work each night and spend time with my son."

Some of the parents in the small audience applauded as Dr. Caldicott smiled at the speaker. "Thank you for that, John. Anyone else care to share?"

An attractive woman stood up. "Um, Dr.

Caldicott, I don't know if you remember me. I'm Judy Effkin."

"Of course, Mrs. Effkin," Dr. Caldicott said, beaming. "Andy's mother."

"That's right." She coughed politely. "Well, this may sound strange . . . but although we couldn't be more pleased with Andrew's improved studies, he's become somewhat, oh, *different,* since returning from your weekend Enlightenment Seminar."

Dr. Caldicott waited. When she did not continue, he asked gently, "Different? How?"

Judy Effkin said uncertainly, "He's become somewhat cruel?"

A few of the parents muttered, but Dr. Caldicott seemed unperturbed. "Cruel? How so?"

Andy's mother looked uncomfortable, but she forged ahead. "I can't explain it. Only that he's . . . unkind. . . to almost everyone outside the club."

Some of the parents nodded in agreement.

Dr. Caldicott stood up, warming the entire room with his smile. "I can understand your concern, and let me address it. Kids being kids, we've found that they go through a brief period of being 'snobby' after one of our seminars. But do you know what it is? It's a feeling that's new to them—it's called pride. We teach them things at the Enlightenment Seminar that will set them on the path to excellence. Their thinking is better, their work habits more structured—they're improved. These kids are reaching a higher place. And if, for some reason, they become impatient with those who don't see things as clearly . . . well, when you soar with the eagles, the pigeons below can seem a bit pedestrian."

Judy Effkin started to fade under his smile. "But . . . this is my son. . . ."

Caldicott nodded. "And he's part of you. Twenty-one years ago my wife, Mary, gave birth to our daughter. And at the moment of birth, I had to touch every inch of her. Ten fingers, ten toes. She felt—and was—perfect."

Gavin and Steve glanced at one another. What was he talking about?

Caldicott continued, "And I made a solemn vow that from that day forward she would always be perfect." He looked suddenly pained. "But the world in which we live does not cherish perfection. By the time she reached her teens, my daughter was out of control. And I felt like you. Helpless. But I refused to let go. I devoted every ounce of my being to helping her. And today, I'm proud to say, she's been accepted into the veterinary medicine program at Stanford; in a committed relationship with a young San Francisco district attorney; and bakes a Toll House cookie that makes you see God."

He turned his smile on Judy Effkin again. She started to say something, then closed her mouth. With a small nod, she sat down.

Dr. Caldicott turned to the stack of papers in his hand. "Now, our next order of business. A new candidate has been nominated. Parents have been counseled and have consented. Miss Perkins, if you will."

Miss Perkins read facts off a sheet in her hand. "Male. Seventeen years old. Suspended four times last year, written up on a dozen occasions this year; parents claim he spent the summer using drugs, alcohol, nicotine. Parents feel he's depressed, spending far too much time listening to rock music and masturbating."

Gavin snorted. "Sounds like all he needs is a girlfriend."

Miss Perkins droned on. "Candidate has a history of truancy, substance abuse, apathy, and general lack of ambition. He is a C student, yet has A-plus potential."

As she finished, Dr. Caldicott added, "This child is not hopeless—at least not yet. It requires a great deal of insight and courage for his parents to allow the young man this opportunity. All in favor?"

The parents in the audience raised their voices in a chorus of ayes.

"Against?" Caldicott asked.

Silence.

"Candidate confirmed. Training to begin A.S.A.P." Dr. Caldicott motioned to Miss Perkins. "Will you please bring in the parents?"

Miss Perkins walked into the wings. Gavin and Steve watched as she returned, escorting a couple in their mid-forties.

"Oh, Jesus," Gavin gasped.

"What?" Steve asked.

Gavin took off back down the ventilation shaft.

Caldicott introduced the parents. "Join me in welcoming into our circle of friends—Ernest and Lucille Strick."

PART TWO

Don't worry about the snakes in the garden

when the spiders are in your bed. . . .

CHAPTER 13

G avin burst out of the basement window and onto the lawn in front of Cradle Bay High. His heart had been pounding since the minute he'd seen his parents rubbing elbows with the Blue Ribbon parents.

"What do I do?" he said frantically. "I can't go home. 'Training to begin A.S.A.P.' You believe this crap?"

Steve tried to calm him down. "So they want you to join their club. Big deal. You shine them on. Blow them off. What can they do?"

Gavin stopped, then yelled right into Steve's face. "You still don't get it. You still think this is about bake sales and blood drives!"

Steve backed away, feeling his face flush. "I'm going home now, Gavin."

"I don't think you are!" Gavin reached into his jacket pocket and pulled out something dark gray, cold, and heavy.

Steve knew exactly what it was. The sight of the gun triggered a flashback, and for a moment he no longer saw Gavin, or Cradle Bay High School at night. He saw a park in Chicago, two dead bodies, and a gun lying between them.

Steve shook the memory from his head and backed away, but Gavin wasn't pointing the gun at him. He was waving it toward the school.

"Where'd you get the gun, Gavin?"

"It belongs to that jerk I call Dad. Now, let's go."

"Put the gun away, Gav."

Gavin hesitated.

Steve took a step toward him. "Put the damn gun away. I'll go with you. Just put that thing down."

Gavin blinked, took a breath, and slipped the gun back into his pocket.

"Okay," Steve said, relaxing only a fraction. "What do you want to do now?"

"*Habeas corpus,* my friend," Gavin said weakly.

"What's that?"

"It means 'produce the body.'"

CHAPTER 14

Before moving to Cradle Bay, Steve Clark had never broken into anything in his life. Now he found himself breaking and entering for the second time in one night. And he didn't like the direction his new career in crime was taking. First a B & E at the high school.

And now the morgue.

After stopping at the school's auto shop to pick up a crowbar, Gavin led Steve across town to the hospital. Actually, they didn't have to break into the hospital building itself, as it was open twenty-four hours, and once they were inside, it was easy enough to take the elevator down to the basement. After all, in a small town like Cradle Bay, who was going to raid a room full of dead bodies?

The only real obstacle they encountered was the lock on the morgue door. Gavin took care of that with one stroke of the crowbar. The lock fell to the floor with a clank that echoed down the hallway. They stopped, listening. No alarm sounded. No one came.

Satisfied that they wouldn't be interrupted, Gavin carefully reached through the shattered glass to open the door from the inside.

They entered the morgue. Gavin hid the crowbar under a hallway table, then tiptoed down the corridor, passed through one set of doors, and crept forward to the refrigerated storage room.

"This is it," he whispered.

He opened the door.

Inside the refrigeration room lay only one body—that of an elderly woman, gray and emaciated.

Gavin looked almost as pale as the corpse. "Mary Jo Copeland—she's not here."

Steve shrugged. "Maybe she got up and walked out."

"Screw you. She's gotta be here somewhere."

Gavin brushed past Steve and returned to the main corridor. The autopsy room where they'd viewed the drunk driver with their class was empty. Beyond it lay another storage area marked BIOLOGICAL WASTE.

"Uh, that doesn't sound like a great place to hang," Steve said.

Gavin ignored him and opened the door. The bio-waste room was dim, lit only by a few yellow emergency lights close to the floor. Alone, he took a few careful steps into the room and felt along the walls, looking for a light switch. Nothing. He took another step. Something tripped him and he went over in a heap, crashing into a shelf. Jars and bottles rained down on him, clattering on the cold tiled floor. One jar landed in his lap and he picked it up.

In the dim yellow haze of the floor lights, he saw an eyeball floating in the jar of liquid. It bobbed up and down, then settled to stare at him. Gavin dropped the jar.

"You're gonna wake the dead," Steve whispered from the door.

"You're funny—like the plague," Gavin replied, trying to stand up. His feet were caught on something.

"What's in the bag?" Steve asked.

Gavin realized that he'd tripped and fallen on top of a body bag. He was standing on someone's corpse. He jumped straight up in the air and landed spread-legged, trying not to touch it.

But through the semitransparent plastic of the bag, he saw that the figure inside looked female. Gritting his teeth, he ran his hands along the body until he felt the toe tag through the plastic.

"'Jane Doe,'" he read.

He stood up and stepped back, his knees turning to water. "Screw this, man. I can't. Let's bail."

Steve met him halfway between the corpse and the door. "No, no. We're here. Let's end this. Once and for all."

The two of them moved back to where the body bag lay. Steve swallowed, trying to keep his heart from leaping up into his throat. He reminded himself that he'd seen a dead body before. This couldn't be any worse than that. Nothing could be worse than what he'd seen back in Chicago.

Slowly he started to unzip the bag, revealing the corpse's feet and ankles.

"The left one," Gavin whispered. "Her tattoo was on the left one."

Steve looked at the corpse's left ankle. In the spot where a tattoo might have been, a square of skin had been peeled away. Steve shuddered. He unzipped the bag the rest of the way.

What he saw looked like something out of a butcher's shop. The corpse's hands had been cut off and the arms sewn closed at the wrists. The internal organs were gone, leaving only a hollow space inside an exposed rib cage.

And the head was missing.

"Oh, God," Steve whispered, gagging.

"Jesus, where's her head?" Gavin said, his voice trembling. "What did they do with her head?"

JAMES MARSDEN *as* *Steve Clark.*

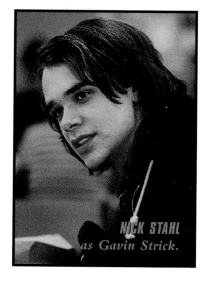

NICK STAHL *as Gavin Strick.*

KATIE HOLMES *as Rachel, the girl from the wrong side of the tracks.*

GAVIN *and* **STEVE** *hang out in the lunchroom.*

RACHEL:
*a girl with
attitude.*

STEVE *shares a smile.*

GAVIN, RACHEL, and STEVE are shocked at what they find in the market.

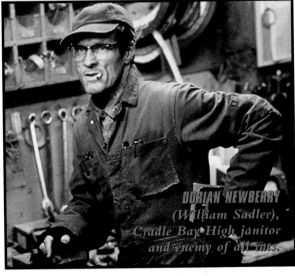

DORIAN NEWBERRY (William Sadler), Cradle Bay High janitor and enemy of all rats.

DR. EDGAR CALDICOTT (Bruce Greenwood) addresses the Cradle Bay parents.

STEVE is shocked by **GAVIN'S** radical change of appearance.

NEWBERRY *recounts the history of Cradle Bay to* STEVE.

RACHEL *and* STEVE *on the run.*

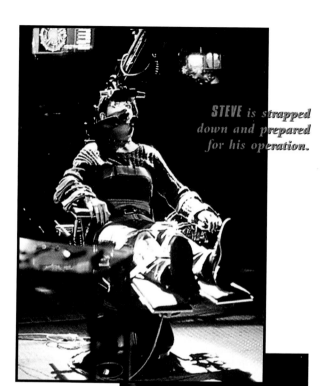

STEVE *is strapped down and prepared for his operation.*

IMPLANT TIME.

Photograph courtesy of Kharen Hill

The stars of

DISTURBING BEHAVIOR:

NICK STAHL, KATIE HOLMES, and JAMES MARSDEN.

CHAPTER 15

Night on the streets of the town was calm and beautiful. The moon drifted over the bay and shined golden on the water. A postcard-perfect moment. Every now and then, in the distance, the sound of a car rose and died away—someone who'd been working the late shift taking the drive home. Otherwise, Cradle Bay lay covered in dreams.

But for Gavin Strick the dream had long since turned into a nightmare, and it was a nightmare he no longer wanted to face. He strode down a residential street, his lanky legs carrying him as fast as possible away from the morgue. He pulled a pipe from his pocket and started to stuff it with pot.

Steve trotted to keep up with him. "Maybe you should lay off that stuff."

"Maybe you should eat me," Gavin snorted. He fired up the bowl and sucked in the pot

smoke as if it was oxygen. "This is huge, Steve.
It's huge. Andy Effkin goes postal. Officer Cox
covers it up. Mary Jo gets chopped up and probably ends up in a can of dog food." He shook his
head and squinted, trying to hold back tears.

They reached an intersection, and each turned
in a different direction. Steve stopped. "Hey,
come this way. Stay at my house tonight."

Gavin wiped his eyes and shook his head. He
straightened his shoulders and pulled the gun
from his waistband. "Uh-uh. I'm going home,
and when I get there, if they're waiting for
me?—I'll tell you what'll happen." He aimed the
gun at an imaginary target. "I'll smoke 'em."

Gavin moved the gun from one imaginary
target to another, firing make-believe bullets.
But his hands were trembling, and Steve knew
that if he pulled the trigger, real bullets would
wind up in a nearby house.

"Gavin," he said as calmly as possible. "Give
me the gun."

He reached forward and took the gun from
Gavin's weak hands. "You're losing it, Gav.
You'll wind up shooting the paper boy. Just go
home."

When Gavin said nothing, Steve gave him a
reassuring pat on the shoulder and repeated, "Just
go home." Steve tucked the gun into his pocket
and headed for his own house.

Gavin blinked. "I woulda smoked 'em all," he said to the empty street.

Gavin trudged up the steps of his front porch. He was hungry, but his stomach felt queasy. He wasn't sure if it was from the pot or the body parts he'd seen in the morgue.

He felt worn out. Beaten down. Ever since he'd seen the murder, he'd felt as if he'd been carrying a lead weight around on his shoulders. At first he'd thought that if he told his friends, they'd help him carry the load. But they hadn't believed him. Even after seeing the Blue Ribbon meeting, Steve hadn't believed him.

Screw them, Gavin thought. *They're worse than Blue Ribbons. Blue Ribbons can't think for themselves. Steve, Rachel, U.V., they just won't even try.*

He opened his front door and heard the TV from the living room. He could see his parents sitting side by side, staring at the screen. He didn't bother to say hello. His parents generally didn't care whether he was home or not.

From the hallway Gavin stared at them for a minute, shaking his head in disbelief. They were his parents. They were supposed to be on his side. "Smoke 'em all," he whispered.

He tiptoed upstairs to his room, opened the door, and walked in.

He never saw the shadows close in behind him.

Downstairs in the living room, Mr. Strick picked up the remote control, increasing the volume until it was loud enough to drown out his son's screams.

CHAPTER 16

BE BLUE BE TRUE!

The banner snapped in the breeze just outside the window of Mr. Rooney's English classroom. Steve stared out the window, his mind several thousand miles and two hundred years away from the eighteenth-century English novel the class was discussing.

Mr. Rooney walked up and down the aisles, dropping essays on desks. "Very nice . . . Very ugly . . . Very mediocre . . ."

He stopped in front of Steve's desk, holding the corner of Steve's essay by the very tips of his fingers. "Very, very, very awful."

Rooney cast a disapproving glance at Steve, then moved on to Dickie Atkinson's desk. He smiled. "Pray tell, Mr. Atkinson. Have you found God? Or a crack term paper service? This paper is exceptional."

Dickie sat taller in his seat. "Thank you, sir."

Steve glanced over at Gavin's desk.

Empty.

When English class ended, Steve bolted for the exit to the school grounds and raced toward Gavin's house. He was out of breath by the time he rang the bell. Mrs. Strick opened the front door but kept the screen door locked.

"H-Hi," Steve gasped. "My name is Steve Clark. I'm a . . . a friend of Gavin's. He around?"

Mrs. Strick pursed her lips. "Gavin is at school. Why aren't you?"

"I was. He wasn't. I thought he might be sick."

Mrs. Strick half closed the door. "Gavin's fine. I think you'd be best to leave us alone. Gavin's a good boy now. He doesn't need bad influences. And that's what you are. You and that . . . that slut from Cook's Ridge. And that pink-colored boy." She slammed the door.

Steve stared at it.

He had sent Gavin home because Gavin had seemed to be losing it.

Now Gavin was in trouble. And the scariest part was that Steve didn't know what kind of trouble.

Steve backed down the porch and started to walk around the side of the house.

"He's not home." Rachel stepped out of the bushes in front of him.

"You know where he is?" Steve asked.

"Nope. I'm just a slut from Cook's Ridge. You?"

Steve shook his head. "I was with him last night. He was pretty wigged out. He got elected into that Blue Ribbon thing."

Rachel nodded, as if that explained everything. "Really? That's it, then. I bet he bailed. Left town."

"But I saw him go home."

Rachel shrugged. "This is *Gav* we're talking about. He went home, grabbed his stash of weed, and hit the road. Mrs. Strick probably just doesn't want to look like a bad mommy."

"You think so?" Steve asked.

"Guaranteed."

Lunch in the Cradle Bay High School cafeteria was exactly the same. And it wasn't. Same pale yellow macaroni and cheese, meat loaf, and peas served by the same sober-faced cooks. Same Blue Ribbon girls in the corner, running a bake sale for some school team. Same kids hanging out at the same tables.

But without Gavin there to liven up the scene, it all looked gray to Steve. He shared a table with Rachel and U.V., picking at his food.

He hadn't said much since they'd returned from the Strick house. He was trying hard to convince himself that Rachel was right about Gavin taking off. He had just about succeeded when, across the table, Rachel dropped her fork.

"Who put acid in my Spam?"

Steve looked up, then followed her gaze to the cafeteria doors.

There, stopped in the doorway as if he was posing for the paparazzi, was a good-looking young man in a pressed oxford-cloth shirt and creased chinos. His hair was cut fashionably short, and he wore a smile meant to warm the hearts of millions.

Gavin Strick.

"Jesus," U.V. whispered.

His entrance made, Gavin strolled forward, brushing past his old friends without even a pause. He headed straight for the Blue Ribbon tables.

Rachel stood.

"Rachel, leave it . . . ," Steve started to say, but she was already on her way.

"Gavin?" she asked when she reached him.

The new Gavin Strick turned and smiled at her. "Why, hello, Rachel."

"What's up with this?" she asked, indicating his clothes and hair.

Gavin pressed a wrinkle out of his shirtsleeve.

"I just want to apply myself. I think I'll get better results on this side of the cafeteria."

Robby Stewart put an arm around Gavin as if they were new best friends. "Why don't you beat it, honey? This is rarefied turf. Sluts need not apply."

"Later, Rachel," Gavin said. He slipped past her and approached the bake sale table.

Steve and U.V. went to talk to him, but Andy Effkin and Trent Whalen blocked their path. "Andy, Trent," Steve said calmly. "Will you excuse us?"

Trent delivered a menacing look at Steve. Violent and eager, Trent's eyes seemed to flash. "You're not wanted. Leave him be."

Andy shoved Steve to the floor.

Trent picked U.V. up and tossed him onto a cafeteria table, sending cups, trays, and food flying in all directions.

Rachel came over. "What's your maladjustment, Effkin?"

Steve jumped to his feet, looking around for help.

But all he saw were Blue Ribbons.

Click.

Click.

Click.

One by one, the doors to the cafeteria closed. And locked.

Click.

Steve glanced behind him just in time to see Miss Perkins close the door to the faculty lunch-room.

He was trapped.

CHAPTER 17

Andy Effkin stalked toward Steve. Frightened and furious, Steve didn't feel like waiting to see what Effkin had in store for him, so he decided to make the first move. He lunged at the Blue Ribbon, knocking him to the ground. Steve threw wild punches, striking Effkin's jaw and nose, but Andy Effkin was bigger and stronger, and he didn't mind the pain. He punched back, leveling a right that snapped Steve's head back. Steve saw the room spin.

A crowd of Blue Ribbons formed a circle around the fight. "Steve! Steve!" Rachel tried to push her way forward, but the crowd wouldn't let her through.

Andy punched Steve in the stomach. Steve felt the air leave his lungs. Another punch smashed into his nose and he hit the floor, blood oozing from his nostrils. His cheek was cut and his lip

was split. More blood. He couldn't move. He
blinked tears out of his eyes in time to see Gavin
Strick standing over him.

"Wh-What happened to you?" Steve
mumbled.

Gavin smiled. "We shall overcome, Steven."

Steve spat blood. "You . . . okay?"

"Better than you," Gavin chuckled. Wearing
a Blue Ribbon smile, he said "Aw, man. I'm
fantastic." He bent closer to his bloodied
former friend. "You want to know what this is
all about, Steven? This whole thing?" He moved
even closer, speaking into Steve's ear. "It's about
bake sales and blood drives, baby!" He dropped
down the final few inches between them and
slammed his knee into Steve's stomach. As Steve
rolled away and gasped for breath, Gavin stood
and walked away, joining the Blue Ribbons, who
were now streaming out of the cafeteria. Gavin
passed Rachel without even seeming to notice
that she had been grabbed by Chug Roman and
one of his friends.

"Let go of me!" she yelled, struggling to break
free.

Dorian Newberry, the rat-fanatic janitor,
staggered in, carrying his mop and pail to clean
up the mess.

Rachel broke free from Chug.

Chug let her go and strode past Newberry,

kicking over the bucket on his way out of the cafeteria. "Retard," he muttered.

Rachel ran to Steve to see how he was, but when he stood, he just looked away from her, humiliated and beaten.

"Steve?" she asked.

Blood dripping from his face, his head throbbing, Steve brushed past her and left the cafeteria. He was done trying to make friends in this damn town.

Over the course of the next week, Steve traveled from home to school and back again, speaking only when spoken to, stopping only when he had to stop. The bruises on his face rose into massive lumps, then turned purple and black before finally fading. When his parents asked him what had happened, he told them he'd gotten into a fight with some dropouts away from school grounds—he knew none of the students at school would back up his story that the Blue Ribbons had attacked him. When his teachers asked him why he wasn't doing his homework, he said he hadn't been feeling well. He gave whatever answer would get him out of the conversation as soon as possible. It didn't matter if it was true, as long as it was easy and got people to leave him alone.

In the hallway, a group of Blue Ribbons held

up the newspaper, smiling their moronic grins. The front page read: "Cradle Bay High School Graduates Notch 14% Improvement in SAT Scores." Beneath the headline was a picture of Edgar Caldicott.

Steve walked by them, his face tight, eyes averted.

"Steve."

He whirled around. Rachel was standing behind him.

"What do you want?"

Rachel shrugged. "Oh, I dunno. A return phone call? An answered locker note? How about a goddamn break!"

Steve shook his head. "I've got nothing to say."

He started to walk, but she kept pace with him. "Why are you blaming what happened to Gavin on me and U.V.?"

He kept his eyes straight ahead. "It's not about blame. I'm just keeping to myself. It's better that way."

Rachel cut him off, stepping in front of him. "He was my friend too."

Steve continued forward. Rachel started walking backward so that she could look him in the eye. "Listen," she said in a hushed voice. "There's a Blue Ribbon meeting tonight. We should check it out from the nosebleed seats."

Steve shook his head. "You want to continue Gavin's crap, you do that. I just want to walk."

She stopped and let him step around her. "Yeah, and while you're sugarcoating everything, go ahead and squirt some chocolate syrup in your Coke!"

Steve had managed to work out a routine that kept him out of everybody's way before school, during classes, and after school. But lunchtime was the worst. There was no way he was going back into that cafeteria, but wherever else he sat, he felt exposed.

He finally settled for the one place no one seemed to go, now that Gavin had become a Blue Ribbon: the boiler room.

Steve sat on the floor against a furnace and ate his sack lunch. He looked up when Dorian Newberry shuffled down the steps.

The janitor glared at Steve. "You ain't supposed to be down here."

"I hate the cafeteria," Steve said.

"Everybody hates the cafeteria."

When Steve didn't move, Newberry muttered to himself and sat down, opening his own lunch bag. Steve watched him begin to eat an apple and a chicken salad sandwich. Somehow, eating, Newberry lost some of his frantic behavior. He seemed to have forgotten about the rats—even while eating right in the middle of Rat Central.

"You think the kids around here are weird?" Steve asked.

Newberry took a bite of the apple. As he chewed, the pockmarks on his face twisted into gruesome shapes. "Yeah."

"But they're really smart, too," Steve added. "Test scores are up."

Newberry nodded. "Never can tell, though. Christ was a child prodigy. But so was Jackie Coogan. And he became Uncle Fester."

The custodian reached for his soda. As he did, a frayed paperback dropped out of the pocket of his overalls. Steve looked at the title. "*Slaughterhouse-Five*? By Kurt Vonnegut?"

Newberry shrugged. "The rats."

"Forget the rats," Steve said, leaning forward. "You're eating down here in the heart of rat territory. You read *Slaughterhouse-Five*. You're not babbling like you did before." He blinked. "It's all an act, isn't it?"

Newberry said nothing.

Steve shook his head. "Doesn't it bother you that everyone treats you like an idiot?"

Newberry looked at him a moment and stuck his tongue against the inside of his cheek as if he was trying to make up his mind whether to trust Steve. Finally he said, "Not only does it *not* bother me—I encourage it. I'll gladly drool for the masses, as long as they don't impinge on my privacy."

Steve looked at the custodian, then looked around the room. He heard the echo of his own voice, the way the rustle of his lunch bag bounced around the metal furnaces and down the furnace vents. *Voices carry,* Gavin had said. And Newberry was down here all the time.

"What's going on in Cradle Bay?" Steve asked. "What do you know?"

Newberry collected himself, then let it out like a man who'd been waiting years to tell a story.

He sat forward and spoke in a low voice. "Three years ago, four kids, seniors from this high school, on a Saturday night, got properly squiffed on Daddy's gin. Raced through a red light, smashed into Mrs. Elaine Bosco, a pillar of the community, and her son, eight-year-old Scotty, on their way back from the Yogurt Shoppe. Everybody died. Six people in one wreck. Blood and empty beer cans all along the intersection. That was it—the straw that broke the city's back."

"Scotty Bosco Square," Steve whispered.

"'One heartache is more than enough.'" Newberry nodded. "Yep, pretty soon after, Edgar Caldicott showed up. Blew some ribbons.

Rocked the house." He paused. "Kids don't drive drunk in Cradle Bay no more. Course, they don't laugh or dance neither."

Steve remembered Gavin's claim that kids were being hypnotized. "So something is changing them."

Newberry shook his head. "Something's killing them. They just don't know they're dead."

Steve stared at the pockmarked face staring back at him. "Why don't you do something about it?"

The janitor shrugged. "What can I do? This town sucks for heroes." He flashed a crooked grin. "You looking to be the first?"

CHAPTER 18

Steve continued his routine through the rest of the day: keep your head down in class, speak only if called upon, lie low. After school he had a meeting with Mr. Rooney about revising his term paper, and then a guidance counseling meeting with Miss Perkins to discuss his declining grades.

The meeting with Perkins was tense. Steve was sure he'd seen her shut the door to the faculty lounge the day of the fight in the cafeteria, allowing it to go on. But he couldn't prove anything, so he was afraid to accuse her. She would only deny it, and then the entire school administration would see him as a no-good hood.

He wanted nothing more than to escape her office, but she seemed to have a hundred questions, and asked him to fill out three different career placement tests—each of which gave him totally different suggestions as to what his future occupation should be.

By the time he finally did make it out of school, the sun had set.

Wanting to get home as soon as possible, Steve took a detour off the main road and headed through the woods that ran behind his neighborhood. It wasn't a forest exactly—just a patch of woods that hadn't been cut down because no one had built a house or a road there.

Leaves and pine needles crunching under his feet, Steve walked on, considering what Newberry had said. A drunk driving accident had put the town over the edge, and they'd called in Dr. Caldicott to do something to help the students behave better. But what? The Blue Ribbons sure weren't prisoners of their parents' whims. They had more freedom, later curfews, and more social gatherings than anyone else in the school. What were Dr. Caldicott's Enlightenment Seminars, exactly?

A twig snapped behind Steve, and he froze. He waited, but no other sound followed.

He shook his head, telling himself to calm down. *Twigs snapping in the woods, he said,* mentally kicking himself. *Now, there's something you don't hear every day. Jeez, and I thought Gavin was paranoid.*

"Steven!" A voice drifted through the trees.

He stopped again.

"Steven! Where are you going?"

"Who's out there?" he called into the darkness. "What do you want?"

No one answered.

Steve began walking faster. Then he started into a jog. But the voices kept up with him, more of them, laughing and calling out from the shadows.

"C'mon, Steven. Don't go!"

"Stay and play!"

"We're here for you, Steven."

Steve ran, pushing his way through the trees and jumping over bushes. The tip of a branch whipped past his face and cut him, drawing a line of blood across his cheek. He ignored it as he sprinted faster, leaving the laughing voices behind.

He burst out of the woods and into a clearing crossed by a dirt road. Instantly a pair of headlights pinned him in place. Exhausted, paralyzed by the bright lights, he stood stock-still as a car approached along the road. As it pulled up beside him he saw the roof lights of a police car. He looked into the passenger side window as it rolled down automatically.

It was Officer Cox. "What happened to you?" he asked, his voice full of concern.

"Nothing," Steve said.

The policeman laughed. "Don't tell me you cut yourself shaving?"

Steve touched his cheek. His finger came away wet with blood.

Cox dipped into his pocket and pulled out a handkerchief, handing it to Steve. Then he motioned to the backseat. "Come on, I'll give you a lift home."

Steve glanced back at the woods, where the voices had gone silent. He was sure they were still out there. Waiting.

He got into the backseat of the police car and pressed the handkerchief to the cut on his face.

Cox steered down the dirt road and toward the main streets. "So," he said, glancing at Steve through the rearview mirror. "You like our chances against Perry Meridian on Friday?"

Steve shrugged. "I don't know."

Cox smiled, but in the reflection in the rearview mirror, Steve could see that the officer's eyes were still cold and observant. "You're not too big on school spirit, are you?"

"I guess not." Steve pointed as they passed the street that led to his house. "I live on—"

"I know where you live," the police officer interrupted. "This is a shortcut." He paused. "You like it here?"

No! Steve wanted to shout. *You're all a bunch*

of wigged-out lunatics! Aloud, he said, "It's okay." He stared out the window. Where were they going? He didn't recognize these streets.

Officer Cox nodded. "You came to Cradle Bay at the right time. A few years back, it was hell. Kids running wild, vandalism, drunk driving, drugs, the whole enchilada."

Steve decided to do what he'd been doing all week long. Play dumb. "What happened to change it?"

The policeman shrugged. "Things have a way of changing."

Steve stopped looking out the window long enough to glance forward into the front seat of the police cruiser. On the dashboard he saw a small framed picture—a wallet-sized version of a high-school portrait. He recognized a face he'd seen before. One of the Blue Ribbons. A Blue Ribbon who, Steve realized with a shudder, bore a striking resemblance to Officer Cox.

The officer glanced around at Steve. "The same way good things can go bad, bad things can turn around for good." The car stopped. Cox smiled. "Home sweet home."

Steve looked up. If he hadn't been sitting, he would have collapsed in relief. He was home. Officer Cox really had taken him home.

The policeman got out of the car and stepped back to the passenger side. Steve reached for the

door handle—but there wasn't one. There were no
door handles in the backseats of police cars. The
doors could only be opened from the outside.

Officer Cox leaned close, smiling at Steve
through the window. "We work hard to make
things better around here. We wouldn't want
things to get worse again. We understand each
other?"

Steve stared back at him, equal parts of anger
and fear roiling in his stomach. He wanted to say
something that would wipe the grin off Cox's
face, but he was trapped inside the car. "Yes, sir,"
he said at last.

Cox nodded and opened the door.

Steve held out the handkerchief.

"Keep it," the officer replied.

Steve hurried into the house, slammed the
door, then peered through the front curtains.
Officer Cox remained outside for a minute; then
he slipped behind the wheel and drove off.

"Hello, Steven."

Steve whirled around, his heart nearly
stopping, to find himself smiling into the
angelic face of Lorna Longley. She was wearing
a very short skirt and a tight blouse, and she was
standing very close to him.

"What are you doing here?" he managed to
gasp.

She pointed over her shoulder to a few

books and papers spread out on the dining room table. "Helping Lindsay. I'm tutoring her in algebra."

"Where is she?"

Lorna took a step forward, one finger twining itself around and around in her hair. "She's upstairs. Sleeping."

"My parents?"

Lorna smiled. Her eyes were moist. Her lips were moist. He could smell her perfume. "At a meeting."

"What meeting?"

"Oh! You've got a cut!" Lorna exclaimed.

She stepped even closer, so close he could almost feel her brush against him. Gently she took the handkerchief from his hand. She folded it and dabbed the tip against her tongue, then gently wiped the blood from his cheek.

Steve felt his head go light with the scent of her perfume. He tried to resist the urge to lean forward and kiss her full lips.

"Maybe," he managed to say, "maybe you'd better go."

She took one short step back. He could still feel an electric current leaping off her skin, reaching for him. "Is that what you really want?"

No, he thought. "Yes," he said.

She smiled, sensing his confusion. "I'll just use the bathroom first."

She turned away, sashaying seductively down the hall toward the bathroom door. Steve felt his head clear. He dashed into the kitchen to grab a soda, rubbing the cold can on his forehead before taking a long swig. He finished the can, but Lorna still hadn't come out of the bathroom.

"Lorna?" he called out.

He walked down the hall to the bathroom.

The door had been left open a few inches. "Lorna?" he said again. Then he looked inside.

Lorna Longley had been waiting for him. She smiled seductively and, holding his gaze, she unbuttoned her blouse. Her lips were parted, and her forehead shined with perspiration.

"What are you doing?" he asked.

She popped another button. "I'm not sure, really," she purred.

"Go home, Lorna."

Lorna stuck out her lower lip and said softly, pronouncing each syllable, "Don't you find me the least bit attractive?"

Steve shrugged. "I find you extremely attractive. But you're a Blue Ribbon and I'm not. So I don't think we're compatible."

In answer, Lorna lunged forward, pressing her mouth to his, her hands grabbing him around the waist and pulling him close to her.

For a moment he was lost in her kiss, in the feel of her body.

But then he remembered who she was, and what had happened to Gavin. He opened his eyes and found her eyes open too, staring back at him. There was a blankness in her gaze. The passion that was in her body didn't seem to reach any deeper.

As he observed her, Steve noticed a weird wedge of light in her left eye.

He broke away. "Wait a second."

He pushed Lorna back a step, extinguishing the sudden fire between them. Now he could see that the blank gaze in her eye was accompanied by a manic look on her face. Her left cheek twitched.

"Lorna, what's wrong?"

Lorna turned away from him, staring into the mirror. She pressed a hand to her left eye and pushed in as if she was trying to squeeze away a headache. She shook her head, her face contorted in anxiety and fear. "I know I'm not supposed to be doing this. It's wrong. It's bad. It's bad-wrong. Wrong-bad!"

Steve swallowed. "Actually, it's not bad, Lorna. It's normal. It's just that you and I—"

He never finished his sentence. Without warning, Lorna Longley slammed her forehead into the bathroom mirror. Glass shattered and fell into the sink. Steve, looking at the mirror rather than at Lorna, saw her reflection in the broken glass, her image splintered into a hundred bloody fragments.

She snatched up a jagged piece of glass from the sink and turned toward him. "Wrong-bad. Bad-wrong!" She lunged at him, aiming her makeshift weapon at his neck. He grabbed her wrist with both hands, but the fury of her charge knocked him off his feet, sending him to the bathroom floor. Lorna threw herself down on him, the glass shard raised. Steve struggled to keep her from driving the glass into his throat.

Screeching in fury, Lorna reached down and bit him on the chest, ripping the buttons out of his shirt with her teeth. Steve shouted in pain and drove his knee up into her torso. Lorna doubled over, dropping the glass shard as she clutched her stomach.

Steve rolled over and jumped to his feet, expecting her to come after him. But instead she lay twitching on the ground. Her eyes rolled back in their sockets, her tongue hung out, and spit lathered in the corners of her mouth.

"Goddamn," he whispered.

And then, as quickly as it had begun, Lorna's fit ended. Her eyes snapped back into focus. She sat up and blinked, then got to her feet. She seemed not to notice the blood on her hands and forehead, her open blouse, or the shattered mirror.

"Oh my gosh!" she twittered. "I have to get home. I've got a big physics exam tomorrow!"

She brushed past Steve, gathered up her textbooks, and walked out of the house.

CHAPTER 19

Go *forward*. That was the Blue Ribbon slogan. That was a good enough reason for Steve to go backward instead.

He sat on the couch in the quiet house. Lindsay had slept through Lorna's weird fit, and he didn't see any reason to wake her. His parents still weren't home.

Go backward. The perfect anti–Blue Ribbon campaign. At least, that was what Steve told himself as he pulled a homemade video from the entertainment center and popped it into the VCR. But deep down he knew that his real reason for watching the tape was that he hadn't gotten over the death of his brother, Allen.

The tape played.

The living room of the Clark household in suburban Chicago. A handsome eighteen-year-old man in an NWA T-shirt walks through the room carrying two sodas. His name is Allen Clark, and he possesses natural good looks that make him at once lovable and likable.

"Hey," he says to the camera, passing by, heading out of the living room and upstairs.

"Hey," says Steve, invisible behind the lens, following.

Allen takes the stairs two at a time. The camera bobs up and down. "Say a few words, Mr. Clark."

"A few words?" Allen laughs. "Screw 'em all and sleep till noon. How's that?"

"Very profound," Steve replies from behind the camera.

Allen stops at the door of his room. "Oh, you want profound? Okay. How about: 'Don't worry about the snakes in the garden when the spiders are in your bed.' You like?"

"Oh, yeah," Steve replies.

"Thank you. Do your viewers care to enter the Cave of the Lovers?" Allen asks.

The camera nods. Yes.

The door swings open, and the camera follows Allen Clark into his room. The appropriate posters color the walls: Chicago Bulls, Soundgarden, and Jerry Garcia.

Sitting on the bed is the most beautiful girl the camera has ever taped. Blond hair, eyes as wide and placid as Lake Michigan.

"Hey, Steve," she says to the camera.

Allen gives her a wet kiss. "Okay, I'll say it for the

folks out there. Sitting next to me is a walking, talking Reason to Continue."

Steven paused the tape. Hit Rewind.
"Sitting next to me is a walking, talking Reason to Continue."
Rewind.
". . . Reason to Continue."
Rewind.
". . . Reason to Continue."

Steve lay in his bed and woke to the sound of gunshots. He sat bolt upright, his body covered with sweat. He listened for more gunfire but heard none. A moment later he realized that he'd heard them only in his head. He'd been dreaming.

He'd dragged himself up to bed after watching the video of his brother a dozen times. It was the last video ever shot of Allen—taped only a few days before he died.

It was only five A.M., but Steve knew he wouldn't be able to sleep. Putting on his robe, he staggered downstairs and into the kitchen. He was pouring himself some orange juice and looking out the window when he saw his father sitting on the porch, staring out into the growing light of morning.

Steve opened the back door. "Dad?"

His father watched the sun begin to peek over the distant mountains across the bay. "Isn't it beautiful? Chicago never had this." He looked back at Steve. "What happened to the mirror?"

Steve drank his juice. "Oh . . . just an accident. I'll fix it after school."

"Sure," Mr. Clark said, returning to his study of the sunrise. "Easy fix." Suddenly he tossed his glass out into the darkness. A moment later Steve heard it thump to the ground.

Steve gazed at his father. "What's wrong, Dad?"

"Nothing. Nothing's wrong."

"Uh, how was your meeting last night?" Steve asked.

"Fine," Mr. Clark said. "It was at Lindsay's school. They showed us everything. Parent indoctrination, the works."

Indoctrination . . . Steve wondered what that was supposed to mean. He looked at his father, unsure why he was acting so strangely. He shrugged to himself. "Okay, Dad." He moved to go.

"Hey . . ."

Steve stopped, looked at his father's back as he watched the sun spread light over the water, reaching toward Cradle Bay. "Yeah?"

Mr. Clark turned to face Steve. "I love you,

son. And there's nothing we wouldn't do for you, and Lindsay. . . . Nothing we wouldn't do to help you. . . ." He turned away and looked back to the sunrise.

Perplexed, Steve stepped back into the house.

CHAPTER 20

Rachel and U.V. dodged their way down the school hall like two squirrels on a busy highway. All around them Blue Ribbons walked straight from class to class, threatening to trample anyone who got in their way. When Rachel had been at her locker that morning, Caldicott had passed and she'd noticed him glowering at her. It had been completely unnerving.

"C'mon, get over it," U.V. said. "Bail on class and go with me. I gotta sell this bud . . . I got like two customers left. This keeps up, I'm 7-Eleven guy."

Rachel shook her head. "I gotta grab a smoke. Catch ya." She ducked through the doors to the boiler room.

Down in the basement, Rachel went over to the unused furnace and reached inside, hoping to find Gavin's smoke stash. Instead she felt something square and smooth. Pulling it out, she found herself holding a compact disc in its plastic case.

"Come out, come out, wherever you are!"

Rachel jammed the CD into her pocket and spun around to see Chug Roman standing at the bottom of the stairs. He grinned. "I saw you come down here, Rachel. I saw the look of a tried-and-true nicotine fit on your face."

She backed away into the shadow of a furnace.

The beefy-faced football player took a few steps forward. "I just want to ask you something." His eye twitched. "I just want to know if . . . hope you don't mind me askin' . . . my friends'd never . . . uh, Rachel, will you go out with me?"

Her jaw nearly hit the basement floor. "You're kidding, right?"

"Will you?"

Rachel shook her head. "No, Chug, I won't."

Suddenly he reached forward and grabbed her by both arms, shoving her against a wall. "Why not?" he demanded.

She met his gaze evenly and watched in fascination as the twitch in his left cheek got faster and more violent. "How about this: You couldn't repulse me any more if you were equal parts crap and maggots."

Chug put his face closer, so close that she

could feel his warm breath. "Okay, then. You want to be that way, I'll be this way." He kept her pinned against the wall with one hand while the other pawed at her breasts. Rachel struggled, but he was far too strong for her.

"I'll scream!" she threatened.

Chug laughed. "What do you think will happen if you do? I'm a Blue Ribbon. Team captain. You're a trashy tattooed love doll."

"Bastard!" she cried.

Something flashed in his eye. "Come on, baby. Give up the plate. Give up the plate for old Chug." He tore her top down from one shoulder, then started to pull at her jeans.

"No!" Rachel shouted.

Chug didn't care and began unbuttoning his own jeans, dragging Rachel down to the floor.

Suddenly a high-pitched shriek filled the basement.

It was only loud enough to make Rachel's ears tickle. But to Chug, it was excruciating. He released Rachel and pressed his hands to his temples as if he was trying to keep his brain from exploding. Chug howled and threw punch after punch at the walls.

Free, Rachel got to her feet and sprinted out of the boiler room.

In a rage, Chug looked around, desperate to find the source of the sound. He spotted a blinking red light on a black box taped to a pipe near the ceiling. The red light pulsed to the high-pitched squeal.

With a roar, Chug jumped up and struck the box, hitting it again and again until his hands started to bleed, pounding until the box came loose from the pipe and crashed to the floor. The football player raised one foot and stomped on the box. The red light died.

Instantly Chug stopped. He heaved a deep breath. His eyes focused. He looked around.

Newberry, the custodian, stepped out of the shadows. Chug glared at him. "What are you lookin' at, retard?"

Newberry put his head down. "Nothing."

"Thought so." Chug lumbered past the janitor and headed up the stairs in time to collide with Steve, who was just heading down to the boiler room, lunch bag in hand. Steve stopped, staring at Chug's bloody hands.

Chug scowled. "Watch yourself, weak tool." Then he was gone.

"What's going on?" Steve asked Newberry.

The custodian was down on one knee, picking up the pieces of his smashed device. "Funniest damn thing," he muttered. "This . . . this rat box. It does something to them. To the Blue Ribbons."

"Does what?"

Newberry shrugged. "I'm not sure. But whatever it is that makes them the way they are—smart and all—this thing, when they hear it, it makes them mad as weavers."

CHAPTER 21

Steve decided to wait for his sister at her bus stop. He wasn't sure why. Maybe it was just that he didn't have any friends of his own, and somehow, after a day surrounded by the hostile expressions of the Blue Ribbons at school, he wanted to see her friendly face.

As the bus pulled up, Steve saw that almost all the kids sat facing forward, quiet and well-behaved. One little boy stared out at him. The kid was no more than ten, but he wore a serious expression and hardly even blinked. This was nothing like the rowdy, chaotic school buses Steve used to take to and from elementary school.

"What are you doing here?" Lindsay asked as she jumped off the bus. Her friend Shannon followed.

"Can't a guy walk his sister home?" Steve nodded to Shannon. "How you doin'?"

Shannon groaned. "Doing! *D-O-I-N-G!* That's an easy one."

Lindsay leaned close to Steve and stage-whispered, "Shannon has spelling bee troubles."

"Shannon!" a voice called from the distance. Shannon waved to a smartly dressed woman standing beside a station wagon. The woman waved back, eyeing Steve suspiciously. Shannon waved goodbye to Lindsay and Steve and took off with her mom.

Brother and sister walked the six blocks to their house. Steve started asking Lindsay about her day, but she, like any nosy little sister, got right to the point. "You hate it here, don't you?"

Steve paused. "It's just . . . different around here. The kids—"

"The kids are weird," Lindsay said matter-of-factly. She used her index fingers to push up the corners of her mouth in a fake smile. "They're always happy. They're always smiling. They're like those chipmunks on the cartoons. Chip 'n' Dale. It's a whole town of Chips 'n' Dales. Yeah." She rolled her eyes. "But they're okay. They're nice and smart."

"They are smart," Steve agreed.

Lindsay pursed her lips, and Steve could see that she was trying to figure out how to say something. Finally she just blurted out, "Steve, I

think you should just try and fit in. 'Cause we're
here for a long time. Me, you, Mom, Dad . . ."

"Chip, Dale," Steve added lightly.

Lindsay nodded and smiled. She reached to
take her brother's hand, and as she did, her sleeve
rode up and he noticed a blue ribbon tied around
her wrist. "Where did you get that?" he snapped.

Lindsay smoothed the ribbon down, scared.
"They were handing them out at school. We all
got one."

Steve stared at the ribbon, about to yank it from
his sister's wrist when a car cruised by. Inside, he
could see Andy, Robby, Trent, and Randi. They
glared at him.

"Go inside," he said to Lindsay.

"Why?" she asked.

Trent Whalen leaned out of the car and
flashed his all-American smile. "Hi, Lindsay!"

Lindsay smiled and waved.

"I said get inside!" Steve planted himself
between the car and his sister, but the Blue Ribbons only laughed, and the car pulled slowly away
and disappeared around a corner. Lindsay gave her
brother a cold look and walked into the house.

Steve waited a few minutes to make sure they
weren't coming back around the block. Then he
went inside.

His parents met him the second he walked in
the door.

"Steve," his mom began.

"What?" Steve replied.

His father stepped forward and said sternly, "A Dr. Caldicott from the high school called today."

"What did he want?"

Mrs. Clark continued, a note of concern in her voice. "He said you've been ditching, that your grades have plummeted since we moved here, and that your new friends leave much to be desired."

"What friends?" Steve said sarcastically.

"This is serious, Steve," his father warned.

"Yes, very serious, Dad," Steve answered, getting irritated.

Mrs. Clark's shoulders slumped. She looked as if she wanted to hug him. "Don't do this, Steven. We're trying to establish ourselves and make a new home."

"This isn't my home."

"We left Chicago for a reason," his mother insisted, "and we're all getting along here just fine. Lindsay's adjusting. We're all happy here. Why can't you be happy too? Why do you have to be the exception?"

"Just exceptional, I guess," Steve said. He stepped around them and saw Lindsay listening from the stairway. He looked away from her and headed through the house and out the back door.

The Cook's Ridge trailer park lay on the south side of Cradle Bay, on the crest of a hill overlooking what had once been a strip mine. Trailers in various degrees of disrepair sat haphazardly all around the park.

Steve found the address he was looking for and knocked. When Rachel opened the door, he could see she'd been crying. "What happened?" he asked.

"Nothing. Forget it," she answered.

He sensed he shouldn't force the issue. "Listen, we need to talk."

"Damn straight," she replied, wiping her nose. "Your Rebel Without a Friend crap is getting old."

She opened the door wider, and he stepped inside.

"Your mom home?" Steve asked.

"Out working a double shift today," Rachel answered.

The trailer was decorated in Early American junk. There was an ancient TV that was probably black and white. Elvis Presley collector's plates hung on the walls for decoration, and ashtrays stood everywhere. Rachel led him through the tiny living room and into her bedroom in the back. There was almost no furniture—just a bed and a desk. But a whole wall of shelves was stacked with tapes and CDs, and on the desk was a beat-up computer surrounded by floppy disks and stacks of folders.

Rachel pointed at the folders. "College apps. Graduation rolls around, I'm outta here. Cook's Ridge, Cradle Bay, Blue Ribbons, all history."

She dropped to her knees and reached behind her desk, into a hiding place. She pulled out a CD. "I found this in Cancer Corner."

She popped the CD into her computer and double-clicked it. A frame appeared on the computer screen, and a still image of Gavin appeared in the middle of the frame. Behind Gavin, Steve could see rows of computers and printers. He had obviously taped this in the school's computer lab. After a moment the image of Gavin began to move and the audio kicked in. Gavin—the *old* Gavin—spoke.

"Hey, Rach. Gavin Strick here, live and unplugged. I guess if you've found this and I've tossed my Rage records and joined the debate team . . . then you know. Am I hangin' with Trent and Robby and the rest of the Robots? Am I capable only of straight A's and sadism? God, I hope not, but if I am . . ." he trailed off, then continued, "Well, anyway, here's the dish. I hit the vents last night. Heard Caldicott talking to some wonk who mentioned "Bishop Flats Eleven." Then Caldicott freaked on the guy, kicked him out of his office. So I figured something's up with that, right?"

On the CD, Gavin laughed. "Keep an eye on U.V., will you? Though I figure they'd never want someone so pigmentally challenged." He looked at something offscreen. "I gotta split. Love ya. This is Gavin Strick reporting from the Reconstruction!"

The image of Gavin froze on the screen again.

A tear ran down Rachel's cheek. "I really miss that little bastard."

Steve stared at the frozen image of Gavin Strick the way he used to be—half-stoned, wise-cracking, but alive and—at the very least—original. "So we should find out what this Bishop Flats is."

"Way ahead of you, Junior G-man," Rachel said. She snatched a pile of papers from her printer's tray. "I pulled some information off the American Medical Association database. Caldi-cott's last place of employment was a place called the Belknap Psychiatric Facility. He spent seven years doing neuropharmacology, which is a fancy word for—"

"Mindbending," Steve said. "So where's this Belknap place?"

Rachel nodded toward the east. "Just across the bay. In Bishop Flats."

CHAPTER 22

Lorna Longley's body lay stretched out on an operating table. Two doctors in gowns and masks bent over her, connecting several electrodes to her head. They moved and spoke over the rhythm of a heart monitor that pulsed steadily in the background.

A female doctor shined a penlight into Lorna's left eye, then noted, "Parietal lobe activity reads normal. Electrical cortex stimulation pathway intact."

The female doctor checked the readouts on a nearby monitor. "I found that excess stimulation amplifies limbic activity, executive function diminishes, and cortisol levels go through the roof. Do you concur, Dr. Caldicott?" she asked, looking at the other surgeon in the room. "After all, it's your study."

Dr. Caldicott nodded. "Every time one of these kids gets a hard-on, they go out and beat someone with it."

In the shadows beyond the operating table lights, three figures stirred. "Dr. Caldicott, may we have a word, please?"

Caldicott tried not to jump. These men were so silent, so still, that he sometimes forgot they were around at all. He held up his hand a moment and turned back to the other surgeon. "Cut a craniotomy flap. I'll get elbow deep, see what happens."

The female doctor's eyebrows rose over her mask. "But, Doctor, that will mean permanent damage. We could save this girl—"

Caldicott waved her off. "You've got to cut the bruises out of the banana."

As the other doctor continued working, Caldicott pulled down his mask and stepped toward the three figures. They waited, saying nothing.

"We're trying to determine the cause of her violent reaction," Caldicott explained. "Part of the treatment was designed to regulate endocrinologic surges. During moments of arousal or emotional conflict, there appears to be an irregularity, a wild-card response—"

One of the shadow men spoke up. "Which threatens to compromise us and the entire project."

Caldicott shook his head. "We've mopped up the mess. There's no threat of exposure. The treatment works, for the most part. With every successive kid, we're getting closer to perfection. I've got a couple of tiny glitches to iron out, and you'll have your prototype."

Another of the shadow men shifted his weight. "Until you've resolved this 'glitch,' we must consider suspending the expansion phase."

Caldicott stiffened. "That's not an option."

The third shadow man spoke, his voice as smooth and sharp as a knife edge. "We believe in you, Doctor, but you're out on a limb. Don't make us saw it off."

At the same moment, the other doctor began to cut away the top of Lorna Longley's skull.

CHAPTER 23

Belknap Psychiatric Facility was a sprawling group of mauve buildings in the middle of an open field. It didn't have the ominous presence of a prison, nor did it have the multiple safeguards of a psychotic ward. Belknap was, in many ways, meant to deflect attention. It was just a place where friends and family sent their mental rejects—people who weren't a real threat but demanded more attention than their relations thought they were worth.

At night Belknap was extremely quiet. The calmer patients were tired from a long day of treatment or stimulation, and the more energetic patients had already been sedated.

Leaving her truck parked halfway up the road, Rachel followed Steve onto the grounds. They chose the largest building but avoided the main entrance, creeping around the back until they found a side door that was unlocked.

As they crept through a dark corridor, Rachel stopped. "Maybe this isn't such a good idea," she said quietly.

Steve tried to sound brave. "Hey, just think of this as our first date," he whispered.

"But we don't even know what we're looking for," she pointed out.

"We're just looking *around*," he repeated for the hundredth time. "To get a bead on what Caldicott might be up to."

Ahead of them, to the left, they could see a guard station, where an old man in a rent-a-cop uniform sat watching television. To the right stood a set of double doors with a sign that read QUARANTINE AREA. AUTHORIZED ADMITTANCE ONLY.

"This is as good as anything," Steve said. Squatting low and pressing against the wall, the pair scuttled down the hallway toward the doors, opened them just enough, and slipped through.

Inside, Steve almost had a heart attack when he saw a man striding toward them. Had they been caught already?

Then he realized that the young man was wearing a bathrobe and blue pajamas, and that he was busy flossing his teeth. The patient hardly seemed to notice them. As he passed, Steve saw blood dribbling down his chin, but still the guy kept flossing.

Steve felt his hand reach unconsciously for Rachel's, and she took it. Together, they crept down the corridor, past a large multipurpose room. Nine people sat around a small television. They were all young—in their early twenties at most. They sat and stared at the TV screen with rapt attention as a woman on a shopping channel described the merits of purchasing a diamond and emerald pendant.

Near them, in a rocking chair, a young woman sat knitting a scarf. It was already at least forty feet long.

In the distance Steve and Rachel heard the *click-clack* of approaching footsteps. They were coming from the corridor.

"Do they know we're here?" Rachel whispered in a panic.

"I don't think so," Steve guessed. "Probably a nurse or something. Come on."

He tried the nearest door. It was locked. So was the next one. Finally they came to an open door and slipped inside, out of sight of anyone in the hallway.

They were in a private room, small but neatly furnished. A young woman sat in a chair in the center, her blond hair flowing past her shoulders. She stared at the wall, not even glancing at them. She rocked herself back and forth and from side to side.

"Meet the musical little creatures that hide among the flowers," the young woman whispered.

"What?" Rachel asked.

The young woman rocked back and forth, ignoring them, whispering, "Meet the musical little creatures that hide among the flowers. Meet the musical little creatures that hide among the flowers. Meet the—"

Outside, they could hear the footsteps grow a bit louder, then stop. They heard voices from a nearby room—the TV room they'd just seen. A moment later the footsteps faded away again.

"Okay, let's go," Steve suggested.

Suddenly the young woman stood up and began to squeal and squawk, flapping her arms in the air.

"Shhh," Steve urged her.

But her voice carried, and soon they could hear patients in the multipurpose room squawking and shrieking too.

"Shut up," Steve pleaded, holding up his hands to calm the woman.

Her shrieking continued, and she began to dance, flitting toward them as she spun around in bigger and bigger arcs. In the other rooms, patients heard her and began imitating her squawks, and the once-quiet Belknap Psychiatric Facility suddenly sounded like a bird sanctuary.

All the patients seemed to shriek in the same ear-splitting tone.

"Oh, God," Rachel gasped over the screaming.

"What?" Steve yelled back.

"I just figured it out," Rachel said. "The floss guy in the hallway, the nine in the TV room, and this one woman. That makes eleven. The Bishop Flats eleven!"

"They're mental patients Caldicott has worked on," Steve concluded.

"Yeah, and we might make thirteen if we don't get them to calm down."

Steve held up his hands again, trying to get the young woman's attention. "Please," he said pleadingly.

Fed up, Rachel stepped forward and punched the shrieking woman right in the mouth. The young woman dropped into Steve's arms like a crumpled flower. The moment she stopped squawking, the other patients quieted too.

Steve frowned. "You get no points for bedside manner."

"But double for saving our butts," Rachel hissed. "Someone's coming!"

They could hear footsteps approaching fast.

"The closet!" Rachel said.

There was a small closet near the bed. Steve carried the unconscious young woman over to her bed and laid her down, then dashed for the closet. Rachel followed, pulling the door after them until it was open barely a crack.

A heavyset male nurse poked his head into the room, glanced at the young woman lying peacefully on her bed, then moved on down the corridor.

Steve and Rachel both breathed a sigh of relief. "Come on, let's get out of here," Rachel said.

"We gotta check and make sure she's okay," Steve said, opening the closet and moving toward the woman.

"I didn't hit her that hard," Rachel insisted.

Steve didn't know exactly what to look for, but she was breathing well enough. He checked her pulse, which seemed strong—and then he froze.

"Rachel," he whispered.

"What?"

He pointed.

Around the woman's slim wrist was a white plastic identification band. The name on the band was Betty Caldicott.

CHAPTER 24

They tore out of the Belknap Psychiatric Facility, trying to be quiet but wanting to get away from there as fast as they could. They sprinted up the road to Rachel's truck. She passed Steve the keys, and Steve started the engine and took off, pushing the gas pedal to the floor.

Only after they'd put some distance between the hospital and themselves did either of them speak.

"His daughter," Rachel spat. "His own daughter. How can anybody not know there's something screwed up in Bishop Flats?"

Ahead they could see an intersection. A left-arrow sign read CRADLE BAY FERRY LAUNCH. A right-arrow sign pointed inland.

Steve took the left to head back to the island.

"Where are you going?" Rachel asked.

"Cradle Bay."

"Are you an idiot?" Rachel demanded. "We should be getting as far away from there as possible." She made a grab at the wheel. Steve shoved her away and slammed on the brakes, skidding to a stop at the side of the road.

"I can't," he said.

She pounded her palms against the dashboard. "If you go back, who's gonna believe you? Your parents? You think they'll believe you about any of this? You think anyone will? Jeez, Steve, I don't even believe it, and I'm right here at ground zero."

Steve sat back. She might be right, but that wasn't going to stop him from trying. He had to do something.

Rachel went on. "You're not the only one suffering here. I waited my whole crappy life to graduate so I could go to college and kiss that crappy little town and its psychos goodbye. And now that's not gonna happen. And then there's my best friend in the whole world, whose brain's been freeze-dried. What the hell am I supposed to do? Where does that leave me? Now all I'll ever be is a forgotten scumbag chick from Cook's Ridge."

Steve looked up. "That's not true."

"No?" she said. "Come on, Stevie boy. Let's disappear. You and me. Nonstop to nowhere."

Steve felt the temptation. Cradle Bay fright-

ened him. The Blue Ribbons frightened him. He
wanted nothing more than to leave them to their
little island and run away.

But one thought held him back.

"I can't. I can't go without my sister."

PART THREE

Go forward. . . .

CHAPTER 25

The ferry was empty except for Rachel's truck. Steve and Rachel sat in the front seat, watching the dark island grow larger and larger across the bow of the boat.

"He was wild, no doubt," Steve said. He'd started talking about his brother. He didn't know why. Maybe it was because he suddenly had so many other mindbenders to deal with that he needed to unload this one—and he needed to unload it on Rachel in particular. "But Allen was also brilliant. I mean, on another wavelength. If he'd made it through his teens, he would've been something amazing."

Steve shook his head. "But he was always in pain. That crazy kind of pain that no one understands except the person feeling it. And Abbey made it go away."

"His girlfriend," Rachel said.

"Yeah. She was incredible. To meet her was to

fall in love with her. But nobody wanted them together. Not my folks. Certainly not hers. I never met two people who were better for each other.

"But for Allen it hurt too much—everyone angling to break them up. So they planned to run away. Go to California or something. The plan was to meet at this playground by the school and then take off. Only, Abbey's parents found out and they freaked. They locked her in her room."

Steve poured out the rest of it, the story he hadn't told anyone since they'd left Chicago. "And Abbey's brother—a real dirtbag named Frank—he drove to the playground. Frank told my brother Abbey wasn't coming. That she had decided to stay, but he should go on himself. Allen lost it. He sat in that playground for hours. Till it got dark. Till a bottle of Jack Daniel's he'd taken from my parents' bar was gone. Till the gun he'd somehow gotten ahold of looked like a good solution to his problems."

Steve swallowed. "So he shot himself. Then, by that time, Abbey had forced her way out of her house and made it to the playground. She found him, and then she used the gun on herself."

Steve felt a tremble start in his jaw and work its way down his neck, into his chest, into his arms.

He pulled his knees up close to keep himself from falling apart. "I was the one who found them. I was the one who had to find them there, lying in the sandbox. And eight months to the day after he died, on what would have been Allen's nineteenth birthday, Dad told us we were moving. To good old Cradle Bay: where everything's going to be all right . . ."

The trembling didn't stop. Steve hugged himself closer, trying to squeeze out the memory of Allen's and Abbey's dead bodies.

He felt a warm hand touch his forehead. He realized that Rachel had moved closer.

"I'm sorry," she said softly. She wrapped her arms around him. He leaned into her and held her close. They looked into each other's eyes, and suddenly they were aware of nothing but each other. They forgot about his brother, about Cradle Bay, about everything but each other. They kissed and held each other tight as the ferry moved ever closer to the dark and silent island.

Cynthia Clark stood outside Steve's room for a long time before she built up the courage to knock. She'd had a difficult time speaking with him lately. He'd become withdrawn, moody, even rude at times. Most of all, he'd clung to the stubborn notion that Cradle Bay wasn't a good

community, wasn't a good home for their
family.

"He'll come around," her husband had
promised.

"But maybe that's the wrong way to look at
it," Cynthia had replied. "That's what we've been
doing, waiting for him to come around to our
way of thinking. Maybe we should go talk to
him, find out what's really bothering him.
Maybe it's not just leftover scars from Chicago.
Maybe there's really something here he doesn't
like."

Nathan Clark scoffed. "What's not to like
about Cradle Bay?"

Cynthia had decided to try anyway. If nothing
else, it would help her open up a dialogue with
her son. She could talk to him the way they used
to talk before their move had upset him.

She knocked. When there was no answer, she
opened the door.

Steve was gone. She checked her watch. After
nine.

At any other time, Cynthia Clark would have
been angry and worried. But Steve had been such
a recluse, staying indoors, leaving the house only
to go to school, that she found herself actually
relieved to see that he'd gone out.

The room itself was messy, and, unable to help
herself, Cynthia set about making the bed. As she

tucked the bottom sheet under the mattress, she felt something and pulled it out.

A gun.

She was holding a gun.

Oh, no. Not a gun. Anything but a gun. She couldn't live through this again.

Cynthia dropped the gun on the mattress. She knew what she had to do.

She hurried into her own bedroom, picked up the telephone, and dialed.

CHAPTER 26

Landing on Cradle Bay, Steve and Rachel headed for the nearest gas station—Frankie's Filling Station, an out-of-the-way self-serve place that suited them fine. While Steve pumped, Rachel studied the ferry schedule.

"Last ferry's at eleven-twenty-five. Just tell me you've got a full-on razor plan, Stevie boy. Just tell me that."

"Oh, hey," he said with a shrug. "I'm just making this up as I go along, okay?"

Rachel smiled, and they exchanged a look.

Steve replaced the pump and screwed the gas cap back on. Before he could get back into the truck, a car pulled into the service station.

A police cruiser.

Through the squad car's windshield, Steve could see the stern face of Officer Cox. "Let's get outta here," Steve said. He jumped into the truck and Rachel started the engine, easing away from the pump.

Officer Cox turned his cruiser, blocking their exit.

"What now?" Rachel asked.

Officer Cox got out of his car, hitched up his weapons belt, and started forward. As he did, the station owner, Frankie Furlong, came out of the shop. "Hiya, Officer Cox!"

Cox cast a quick, hard glance his way. "Closing time, Frankie."

Frankie whirled around like a top. "Yeah. Gettin' late," he said without argument. He vanished inside. Moments later the gas station's lights started going out one by one.

Cox came up beside Rachel's truck. "Past curfew," he grunted.

"She was just driving me home," Steve said. "We were studying."

Cox glanced inside the truck. "Where's your books? What were you studying?"

A pair of headlights shined from the road, momentarily blinding him. The car pulled into the far end of the station lot. Officer Cox kept one eye on Steve and Rachel and one on the newly arrived vehicle, a beat-up El Camino pickup with a bed covered by a tarp. The door squeaked open and a lanky, slow-moving figure stepped out. It was Dorian Newberry, the janitor at the high school.

"Evening, Officer," Newberry said.

"What are you doing?"

"Rats!" Newberry exclaimed. "Getting rid of the rats. Pink-eyed vermin." He ambled past the truck, Steve and Rachel, and the policeman and scrambled down into a culvert in the dark beyond Frankie's station, muttering, "Quarter a rat! Town council pays me a quarter a rat!"

Cox shook his head as Newberry disappeared. "Goddamn moron." He heard a car engine start and turned his attention back to Steve and Rachel. "What do you think you're doing?" he asked.

Rachel played innocent. "Can we go home now?"

Officer Cox had his gun in his hand. "Step out of the car."

"Why?" Rachel asked.

Officer Cox thumbed back the gun's hammer. "Step out of the car."

They started to obey. First Rachel handed Cox the keys through the window, but then Cox opened the truck's door, grabbed her by the shoulder, and dragged her toward his cruiser.

"Hey!" Steve called, following close behind.

The officer held his gun in his free hand.

"Leave her alone," Steve yelled.

Cox ignored him. He shoved Rachel against his car, then opened the door and pushed her into the backseat. He turned and looked at Steve, fingering his gun. "Get in."

Steve wanted to protest, to fight, but he was utterly helpless. He crawled in after Rachel. Cox slammed the door, turned, and—

Thunk!

Steve and Rachel looked out the back window to see Officer Cox dropping to the pavement like a ton of bricks.

Newberry stood behind him, holding a bloodied Ir-rat-icator box in his hands.

"Now, that's a big rat," the custodian said. "Gotta be worth more than a quarter."

He opened the police cruiser's door and let Rachel and Steve out. They had to step over Cox, who lay utterly still, the back of his head oozing blood and brains.

"What do we do now?" Rachel asked.

"Just get out of here," Newberry answered.

Steve gave Newberry a look of gratitude, then glanced at Rachel. "Come on," he told her. They hopped into her truck and took off.

Newberry ambled back to his El Camino with the black box. He peeled back the tarp to reveal a huge collection of Ir-rat-icators.

Rachel cut the truck's headlights and pulled up in front of the Clark house as quietly as she could. Steve nodded and got out, closing the door gently, then lightfooted it across the lawn to the front door. He disappeared inside a moment later.

Rachel counted seconds by the pounding of her heart, and by her count, it was taking Steve a year to get his little sister out of the house.

"Come on, come on," she muttered.

Staring at Steve's front door, she did not notice the figures closing in on her truck.

Steve led Lindsay down the dark hallway, slipping a jacket around her shoulders. Lindsay rubbed the sleep out of her eyes.

"I promise I'll tell you everything in the car," Steve whispered. "But you have to trust me for now. You trust me, don't you?"

Lindsay nodded, too sleepy to speak. Steve held her hand as they hurried downstairs. Before they could reach the door, the lights popped on, momentarily blinding them both.

Blinking, Steve turned to see his parents approaching.

"Where are you going?" his father demanded.

Steve stiffened. "Taking my sister away from here. We're going back to Chicago."

His mother took a step forward, but Steve flinched from her touch. "Steve, you're scaring me," she said.

"I'm scared too. Believe me."

His father said, "Look, Steve. You have to know we're here for you. No matter what."

Steve faced them both. "If you really mean that, then let's *all* go home. *Now.*"

"You *are* home, Steven." Dr. Caldicott appeared from the dining room, stepping between Steve and the front door. "Cradle Bay is where you belong. With your family."

Steve looked from Caldicott to his parents and back. Caldicott had been waiting here. His parents had brought him to their home.

"You signed me up for the program?" he said in total disbelief.

His father held up the gun Steve had taken from Gavin and stashed under his mattress. Nathan Clark's face looked pale and worn. "We're not going to live through that again."

"It's for you, Steve," his mother said. "We just want what's best."

Steve folded his arms across his chest. "What about what I want?"

"Steven," Dr. Caldicott said calmly, "do you like the way you feel right now?"

Steve snorted, cutting him off. He looked at his parents. "You think you can get a smart, well-adjusted kid out of that asshole?" He hurled a scornful glare at Caldicott. "I saw the Bishop Flats eleven. And don't pretend you don't know what I'm talking about."

Caldicott had great self-control. The confident, benign smile never left his face. "I'm not pretending, Steven."

Steve turned back to his parents, unable to decide whether to focus on Caldicott's evil or his parents' betrayal. Finally he said flatly, "You sold me out."

"Steven," his mother pleaded.

"Steve!" he spat back. "My name is Steve. Nobody calls me Steven except for them."

Caldicott gave the Clarks a look of utter sympathy. "I'm starting to understand how difficult it must have been for you."

Steve sneered at him, then pulled Lindsay close. "Come on, Linds." He started for the door. Caldicott held his ground, ready to block their path. Steve gave him a hard look and punched him in the stomach. The doctor crumpled like an old dollar bill.

Steve and Lindsay stepped past the groaning doctor and headed outside.

Right into a crowd of Blue Ribbons.

They formed a semicircle on the lawn, completely enclosing the front of the house. Steve saw all the familiar faces, including Gavin's.

"The Blue Ribbon mother ship has landed," Robby Stewart announced.

"May we have this dance, Steven?" Gavin said.

Steve looked past them to Rachel's truck. Empty. "Where is she?" he demanded.

Gavin and the other Blue Ribbons traded smirks.

Steve bolted forward, wanting to take Gavin's head off. But at the last minute Chug stepped in his way and punched Steve so hard that his feet flew out from under him. Steve hit the ground, and as the night sky started to spin above him, everything went black.

"Steve," Lindsay called, taking a step forward, but Caldicott stepped from the house, took her arm, and guided her back inside.

From the bushes that bordered the Clarks' house, a pale face watched as the Blue Ribbons gathered around Steve and carried him to a car.

U.V. looked from the house to Steve, then back to the house again.

CHAPTER 27

Steve regained consciousness feeling disoriented. He thought the sky was still spinning until he realized that the sky was not sky but a tiled ceiling, and it wasn't spinning.

He was lying on his back on a gurney, moving down a hallway. When he tried to move, he felt leather straps around his hands and feet. He strained against the bonds, but his muscles felt weak. He saw an IV bag hanging from the gurney and guessed he was being sedated.

From somewhere nearby, he heard Gavin's voice. "It's not like you think, Steven."

Steve managed to move his head. He was being pushed by a doctor in a surgical mask as Gavin, Robby Stewart, and Dickie Atkinson followed.

"It's a new kind of cool," Gavin continued. "You become better, freer. I've never felt so alive in my life."

"It's humanity's sacred essence," Robby said.

"A new and finer age," Dickie added.

"Go forward," Robby said.

Steve kept moving his head, trying to clear out the cobwebs. As he did, the gurney flashed past a room where a girl lay unconscious on a table.

Rachel.

Gavin grabbed Steve's face, glared down into his eyes. "Be the ball," he ordered.

Then Steve was being wheeled through a set of double doors into an operating room, and he knew where he was.

Inside the Cradle Bay Hospital.

How many people are involved in the Blue Ribbons' mindbending program? Steve wondered.

Instead of an operating table, the room held a large chair like the kind you'd see in a dentist's office. Over it hung a huge bank of equipment, including a large object that looked like a helmet.

As Steve's gurney was wheeled up to the chair, two technicians loosened the restraints. Steve tried to fight, but he was too weak, and they easily placed him in the chair.

A blood transfusion pouch hung from an IV tree. The printed lettering on the bag read BLOOD DRIVE: CLARK, STEVEN.

They'd been gathering blood from the beginning, planning to put everyone through the process. Whatever it was.

Steve felt the technicians swabbing various parts of his skin, inserting needles. He felt as if he was going to be sick. Beaten up and drugged, he could only lie there as they prepared him for Dr. Caldicott's "enlightenment."

Vaguely Steve heard a door open and close. Then Dr. Caldicott's voice whispered in his ear. "Who have you told?"

"The . . . The world," Steve stammered through a dry mouth. "Geraldo should be here any minute." He fought to clear his head enough to say, "People are going to know when I get out of here."

Dr. Caldicott smiled. "Yes, they will, Steven. They'll know because you'll be better."

The doctor grabbed hold of the helmet-shaped device. Slowly he lowered it until it fit over Steve's head. He set a series of spring-locked steel brackets over Steve's face, fixing the helmet in position.

"That's what this is all about. We've built the better mousetrap. The shrapnel of temptation and excess has so many jagged edges. Adolescence is quite a minefield. But soon—guess what?— you'll be fully equipped to walk right through it."

"Yeah," Steve said, barely able to speak in the confines of the helmet. "Straight A's and a letter jacket. And in exchange, every now and then you rape and kill."

"A glitch," Caldicott said dismissively. "An aberration. To cure cancer, you've got to kill a few white mice, make the necessary sacrifices."

"'Meet the musical little creatures who hide among the flowers,'" Steve chanted.

Caldicott stopped. His neck turned red, but he held his temper and said simply, "That's a battle I didn't win. But you'll be different. I know more now."

He leaned close again. "And to tell you the truth, she wasn't that bright to begin with." He slipped a rubber dam into Steve's mouth, silencing him.

The doctor pulled a small computer disk out of his coat pocket and handed it to one of the technicians. "Steve's parents were very helpful. This should do the trick."

The technician nodded and inserted the disk into a slot in the helmet's control panel. Caldicott smiled at Steve one more time. "Good night, Steven."

Steve lost sight of Caldicott as one of the technicians slid something in front of his face. It was a tiny monitor shaped like a mask, and it hovered no more than a few inches from his eyes. Light flickered in the monitor. Steve tried to shut his eyes but realized that his eyelids were being held open by rubber clamps. Images started to appear in the monitor. Steve's eyes burned as the images got brighter and brighter. He was watching the video of Allen . . . the same video, but somehow totally different. Steve's eyes watered and he clamped down on the dam in his mouth, unable even to scream.

The living room of the Clark household in suburban Chicago. A handsome eighteen-year-old man in an NWA T-shirt walks through the room carrying two sodas. His name is Allen Clark, and he possesses natural good looks that make him at once lovable and likable.

"Do your viewers care to enter the Cave of the Lovers?"

Steven nods. Yes.

The door swings open, and the camera follows Allen Clark into his room. The appropriate posters color the walls: Chicago Bulls, Soundgarden, and Jerry Garcia.

Sitting on the bed is the most beautiful girl the camera has ever taped. She has something in her hand.

"Hey, Steve," *she says to the camera.*

She's holding a gun. She puts the gun to her mouth and pulls the trigger.

Blam! Blood splatters the Jerry Garcia poster behind her as her body drops backward.

Allen gives her a wet kiss. "Sweet girl has become face pizza." *He takes the gun and jams it under his chin.*

"Allen?" *Steve calls.*

Blam! *Brain tissue and gray matter spot the walls. But instead of dying, Allen grins, half the flesh and bone blown off his skull.*

"Hey, dude, go forward!" He lifts the gun, its barrel glistening with blood, and aims it at the camera, at Steve—

And then there is a crackle of static and the scene shifts. The mutilated Allen is replaced by the live Allen, who smiles. "Don't worry about the snakes in the garden when the spiders are in your bed," he says. "Don't worry about the snakes in the garden when the spiders are in your bed. . . . Don't worry about the snakes in the garden when the spiders are in your bed. . . ."

One of the techs studied a readout on the helmet control panel. "Look at this," he said.

The other technician watched the electronic impulses on the screen. "That's odd. Never seen readings like that before. Think it could be a power surge?"

"Maybe," said the first technician. "You stay here. I'll go check the readings on the girl. If her treatment's fine, we'll know there's just something wrong with this machine."

Steve heard his brother's words echo in his mind, drowning out whatever messages Caldicott's machine was meant to send. Allen had lost his reason to continue. His brother, whom he had loved. His brother, who'd been betrayed. Steve refused to meet the same fate. Thanks to those around him, Allen had lost his reason to continue. Steve would be damned if he was going to lose his.

At the edges of the mask's monitor he saw the technician lean over to adjust the equipment. Fighting through the drugs that made his arms feel like rubber, Steve reached up, grabbed a fistful of hair and slammed the technician's face into the steel helmet. He lost his grip as the man collapsed to the ground.

Steve pushed the monitor away, then scrambled desperately to unfasten the spring locks holding his head in place. One by one he unclamped the snaps until he was free. He climbed out of the chair and stood.

His legs were wobbly, but he didn't care. He was free. He set off on a search of the hospital rooms, hoping to find Rachel before it was too late and she had become a Blue Ribbon, one of Cradle Bay's so-called good kids.

In one room he found walls lined with glass-doored refrigeration units. Fluorescent tubes glowed inside, illuminating pouches swollen with blood, each labeled with a name Steve recognized. They were all names of kids from his school and his sister's school. He ducked back into the hallway and continued his search for Rachel. He pushed open another door and found a girl lying atop a gurney.

The girl's face was hidden behind a surgical curtain. Steve shook with fear. The room's only light came from a monitor at the head of the gurney, where a sequence of indecipherable numbers scrolled. Steve slowly walked around the gurney, past the curtain that shielded the face of the girl.

Lorna Longley.

His relief that it wasn't Rachel turned to revulsion when he saw that the top of Lorna's head had been cut off to expose her brain. A dozen needle sensors protruded from the organ, feeding data to the monitor.

Steve shut his eyes, took a breath, then moved on.

CHAPTER 28

The technician leaned over Rachel's helmet, checking the readouts one more time. He'd already looked at them twice and had been satisfied with the numbers. He made his notes and had turned to go back to the new male teen when a shiny steel morgue tool came down on his head, knocking him out cold on the tiled floor.

Steve stepped forward to the chair in which Rachel sat. It was identical to the one he'd been fastened into. He had no idea how to turn the machine off, so he just started unhooking tubes and wires and unsnapping the latches that held the helmet in place.

As soon as the monitor had been removed from her eyes, Rachel blinked. She tried to speak but couldn't. Instead she grabbed hold of him and refused to let go.

"I got you, Rach," Steve whispered. "It's okay. Come on, we're getting out of here."

He lifted her out of the chair and helped her to her feet. Bracing her against him, he staggered out of the room and down the corridor. He tried to remember the layout of the morgue. Somewhere, he was sure, there was an exit that led outside from the basement. Then he turned a corner and saw it—outside streetlights glinting off a glass door at the end of the hall.

They had almost made it out when—

Ka-chunk.

The sound of a soda machine dispensing a can echoed down the hall.

Chug Roman picked up the can and turned, smiling at Steve. He popped open the soda. "Going somewhere with my custard, Steven?"

CHAPTER 29

Steve lowered Rachel to the ground and pulled the steel tool from his pants. "Let us go, Chug."

Chug sipped his cola and laughed. "That's my girl you got there. I can't let you take her, now, can I?"

Chug charged forward like a raging bull. Steve brought the tool down hard, smacking it across the football player's elbow. Chug bellowed in pain but kept coming, driving Steve backward into a wall. Steve thought he felt his ribs crack and dropped the tool. Laughing, Chug wrapped his meaty hands around Steve's throat and squeezed.

Darkness started creeping in around the edges of Steve's vision. He felt as if he was going to lose consciousness.

Thwack.

Steve heard a loud sound like metal striking

stone, and then Chug's hands fell away from his throat. Steve slumped to the floor, but his vision cleared enough for him to see Rachel standing there with the steel tool in her hand. She'd just cracked it across the back of Chug's skull.

The big Blue Ribbon staggered and took a step toward Rachel. She swung the tool again, smashing in the left side of Chug's face. The big ape dropped to his hands and knees, blood pouring from his ruined left eye, but still he kept coming.

Rachel gritted her teeth and raised the tool one more time. She brought it down as hard as she could across the top of Chug's head. The blow made a wet, slapping sound. Chug collapsed, and blood started to ooze around him like a crimson halo. Rachel dropped the tool.

Steve climbed to his feet, and together they pulled each other the last few yards to the exit. They burst through the doors and into the fresh air of Cradle Bay. There was a thin rim of light on the eastern horizon. Morning was coming.

Bright beams of light shined on them as a car pulled up alongside. U.V. was behind the wheel of Rachel's pickup, and Lindsay sat in the passenger seat.

"You guys Blue Robots yet?" U.V. asked.

"Lindsay," Steve said, relieved to see her.

"Naw," Rachel managed to joke, "we can't even get into that club."

"Lindsay!" Steve repeated, smiling.

Rachel went to get into the truck.

U.V. held up a hand. "Not so fast," he said. He studied Steve and Rachel, trying to detect whether they were Blue Ribbons or not. "So," he said, "what's the capital of North Dakota?"

Steve and Rachel looked at each other. Steve shrugged at U.V. "How the hell would I know?" he asked.

U.V. smiled, pleased. "Okay, you're cool. Hop in. We gotta book. The early bird ferry leaves in twenty minutes."

U.V. pushed the truck to its limit, ignoring stop signs and traffic lights, roaring through the early morning. They all leaned forward in their seats, willing the truck to go faster. In ten minutes they reached the road down to the ferry launch.

Steve looked at Rachel. "You okay?"

Rachel leaned into him, her shoulder brushing his. "I dunno. You?"

Steve grinned wearily. "Yeah."

She returned the smile. "Razor."

Suddenly U.V. slammed on the brakes, bringing the truck to a skidding halt. "Damn."

Halfway to the launch, the road was blocked by row after row of cars. Blue Ribbons stood next to each car, waiting.

Engines revved behind Rachel's truck as another car and several motorcycles pulled up to block any chance of a retreat.

Trent Whalen and a few others walked forward. "It's over, Steven," Whalen said. "Your way of praying is over."

Caldicott emerged from the blockade, holding Gavin's gun. His face was as benign as ever. "I'm not here to hurt you, Steven. I'm here to help you. You don't believe it now, but you will—once you've been completed."

Caldicott said something else, but his words were drowned out by the roar of another engine. The Blue Ribbons looked around to see who had started a car; then they realized that the sound was coming from behind them. The Blue Ribbons forming the rear blockade shouted a warning and jumped away from their motorcycles as an old El Camino knocked them over like bowling pins.

Never slowing, the El Camino swerved onto the road and aimed itself right at Dr. Caldicott. The doctor shouted and raised the gun, firing into the windshield of the oncoming truck. The windshield shattered and the truck lurched forward, slamming into Caldicott and sending him flying into a ditch.

The El Camino slid to a stop with Newberry at the wheel. In the back of his truck sat a pile of

Ir-rat-icators, stacked and wired together into the biggest box ever designed to get rid of rats.

The Blue Ribbons who'd been thrown aside by the sudden assault got to their feet and brushed off their clothes. The wedge-shaped light in Trent Whalen's left eye flashed. "It's time to kill a retard."

When Newberry saw the Blue Ribbons start toward him, he flicked a master switch wired to the boxes. Once the connection was made, all the boxes went off at once and the air was suddenly filled with a high-pitched squeal.

All along the road, Blue Ribbons cried out in agony. Some covered their ears. Others tore at their hair.

"Kill it!" Trent Whalen yelled, pointing at the car and its boxes.

The Blue Ribbons started forward, compelled to destroy the source of their pain.

Newberry started up his El Camino and spun it around, heading up a nearby road. He drove slowly enough to punish the Blue Ribbons with noise but fast enough to keep out of their reach.

"What's going on?" Rachel asked.

"He's leading them to the Bluffs," Steve guessed.

U.V. got out of the truck and retrieved the gun Caldicott had held. Steve went to him. "Hey, get Rachel and Lindsay down to the ferry."

"Cool." U.V. climbed into the truck with the two girls and sped off toward the dock.

Steve ran to the motorcycles that had been scattered earlier, found one with the keys still in the ignition, and started it up.

He raced up the road, zigzagging among the tormented Blue Ribbons, until he had pulled alongside the El Camino, which had come to a stop five yards from the edge of the Bluffs.

From behind the wheel, Newberry grinned. "Hey, lunch boy."

"What're you doing?" Steve asked.

Newberry jabbed a thumb at the back of the car. "You like my handiwork? And I said these things didn't work worth spit! Fact is, they bring the rats *out*! And they think *I'm* the village idiot?"

Steve looked at the Bluffs again and realized that the El Camino's engine was still running. He understood what Newberry had planned.

"Don't do this!" he shouted.

Newberry shrugged. "Can't very well have these rat turds graduating and going out into the world, can we?"

Steve glanced at the Blue Ribbons, who were coming ever closer. "They can be helped."

"No, they can't," Newberry said matter-of-factly. "And neither can I."

For the first time Steven noticed the blood-

stain on the custodian's shirt. It started right in
the center of his chest and spread out from there.

The Blue Ribbons neared the car.

"Do good things, lunch boy," Newberry
advised, and shut the car window.

Steve kicked the motorcycle into gear and
swung around just as a crowd of Blue Ribbons
descended upon the El Camino. They crawled
on the hood, into the back, tearing at the equipment, trying to silence the noise that pierced
their brains like knives. From inside the cab,
Newberry watched as the Blue Ribbons worked
themselves up into a frenzy. Trent Whalen and
Robby Stewart pounded their fists on the windows, cracking the glass.

The Blue Ribbons covered the truck like flies
on a piece of fruit. Newberry gunned the
engine, and the El Camino lurched forward,
jutting out into space, then toppling over the
Bluffs. The car bounced and tumbled down the
cliff face, taking the victims of Dr. Caldicott's
experiments with it into the inky water.

Steve watched them fall.

Someone coughed behind him. He turned to
see Dr. Caldicott standing there, one side of his
face scraped into pulp by the car collision. With
the other side of his face, Caldicott smiled.
"Impressive display of previously unsuspected
leadership potential, Steven."

Without another word, the old man and the young charged at each other, locking together like rabid dogs, rolling closer and closer to the cliff's edge. Caldicott was stubborn and smart, but Steve was younger and stronger. He punched Caldicott in the face, then in the stomach. Staggered, the doctor tried to regain the advantage. He launched himself at Steve but slipped forward. Caldicott half tumbled over the edge of the bluff, but he managed to grab hold of Steve's leg, keeping his own upper torso on the ground, his legs dangling in the air below the bluff. Steve fell to the ground and rolled on his back. The weight of Caldicott pulling at him drew him nearer and nearer the cliff's edge.

Steve put his feet to Caldicott's face. "Be the ball," Steve said, and he kicked out, smashing his foot into the doctor's face, once, twice, until Caldicott lost his grip, released Steve, and fell over the cliff.

Steve rode the motorcycle down to the ferry launch. The gate to the ramp was closed, and he could see the ferry pulling away from the dock. Sprinting as fast as he could, he tore across the dock, launched himself at the very last instant, and landed on the deck of the ferry.

The only vehicle on board was Rachel's truck. He hurried over to it and found Rachel,

U.V., and Lindsay standing strangely still and silent.

"What are you guys doing?" he asked.

Gavin stepped out from behind the truck, wearing a set of headphones and carrying a shot-gun in his hand. He pulled the headphones off and let them dangle around his neck. Tinny strains of Mozart could be heard. "Steven! I'm holding your near and dear hostage. I find suffer-ing swell these days."

Steve pointed back toward the island. "They're gone, Gavin. Trent, Andy, Caldicott. All of them."

Gavin shrugged. "Then I guess *I'll* have to be the only New World Man."

"Gavin—"

"Look at you, Steven!" The wedge-shaped light flashed faintly in Gavin's left eye. "You got Rachel, U.V., your sister, the truck. You're like the king of your own little mini-society. The Ayatollah of Coca-Cola. And what do I have? A tweaked brain. A ruined town. But, oh, look, boys and girls, I've also got the gun. . . ."

"Gavin—" Steve called.

Gavin waved the gun at the group. "I want to demystify the process for you, Steven: We live, we die, no one knows why. Okay?"

"Come with us. We'll find a doctor," Steve told him.

Gavin shook his head. "I *had* a doctor. Cald-

icott was a visionary. A genius. He created a psy-
chic jambalaya. Perfect youth. I was honestly beginning to enjoy supervised athletics, chamber
music, and my studies. What's wrong with that,
Steven? Why did you have to screw that up?"

"You're not well, Gavin. Remember what you
used to be like?" Steve asked.

Gavin nodded, tightening his grip on the
shotgun. "Yeah, a drug-addled burnout. A bad
dresser. A shambles with the ladies . . ."

"You're still a bad dresser," Rachel com-
mented.

Gavin scowled. "That was funny . . . once
upon a time."

Rachel smiled, remembering the old Gavin.
"Come with us, Gav."

Gavin waved her off. "Don't you see? I'm a
Ribbon now. There's no going back. I'm just
given to momentary lapses of treason."

"What will you do?" she asked.

"Who knows?"

She pointed to Lindsay, and U.V., and Steve.
"All right then, let us go."

Gavin seemed to consider this. "Okay."

"You mean that?" she asked warily.

"Of course I do," Gavin said, the gleam
returning to his eye. "You should go. All of you.
Go forward! Have a big old party for your pal
Gavin Strick. And call it Life!"

And it almost sounded as if he meant it, but then he raised the shotgun, pumped in a shell, and aimed it directly at Rachel, putting his finger to the trigger.

Three shots exploded across the deck of the ferry, but none of them came from Gavin's shot-gun. All three of them punctured his body, and Gavin went down in a bloody heap.

U.V. stood with Gavin's handgun still smok-ing. Steve took it from U.V., then walked over to Gavin and kicked the shotgun to the side. They all moved to stand beside their fallen friend.

Gavin gasped. "Three times? You hadda shoot me three times?"

"I'm sorry, man," U.V. said. "I really am sorry."

"Yeah, yeah." Gavin coughed. "Stevie boy, I remember the day when I was the leader. Now it's you. I wonder where you'll take them. I gotta tell you: You make some twisted family."

Gavin coughed again, and blood trickled from his mouth. "I gotta tell you, this considerably di-minishes my chances of ever getting to meet Trent Reznor." He paused. "Wow. Maybe I'm coming around."

Those were the last words he spoke. He laid his head back and grew very still, his eyes open and staring up at the sky. In the corner of his left eye, Steve saw something flash, then die out.

U.V. took off his jacket and covered Gavin's face.

Footsteps stamped toward them, and Steve whirled around.

It was the ferryman. He stopped when he saw the guns and the dead bodies.

"Just get us to the mainland," Steve demanded.

The ferryman nodded. "That's what I do." He turned around and headed back for the pilot's wheel. "Back and forth . . . back and forth . . ."

Steve walked to the railing and heaved the guns over the side, watching them splash into the gray-green water. Rachel came and stood beside him. She looked sad, but in the midst of her sadness, she glanced up at him, smiled, and took his hand. The sun rose over the mountains on the mainland, and they both knew they would be there soon.

EPILOGUE

In a crowded auditorium in Chicago's Grand Legion Hall, a crowd of reporters and photographers pressed against the stage to watch the final round of the All-American Spelling Bee.

The moderator motioned for one young girl to stand. "This last word is for the win," the moderator said to the girl. "The word is *phlegm*."

"*Phlegm*," the girl repeated. "*P-H-L-E-G-M. Phlegm.*"

"That's right!" the moderator announced. "We have a winner!"

A crowd of parents and educators in the audience cheered. Camera flashes popped. Video cameras zoomed in, focusing on the face of the junior-high-school girl named Shannon, who stood there, calmly enduring the applause and the cameras, while a tiny wedge-shaped chip flashed in her eye.